All I Want For Christmas Is Two

AMITY MALCOM

Cover Design: Temptation Creations

Formatting: Cruel Ink Editing + Design

Editing: Tiff Writes Romance

To everyone who spends the holiday season dodging their racist, homophobic uncle while escaping with a smut-filled book.

This one's for you.

AUTHOR'S NOTE

As with all works of fiction, All I Want For Christmas Is Two should not be used as a guidebook in any way when navigating the BDSM lifestyle. While not discussed in depth, the topic of parental abandonment is briefly mentioned throughout this story.

Do your research. Be safe. And have fun.

PROLOGUE

I never wanted a sibling.

Never asked my father why it was just him and me, no maternal figure outside of the countless nannies and tutors that came and went on a near-constant rotation, parading around the house like wicked women more intent on winning the affections of my wealthy father than caring for the child left on his doorstep without so much as a note on my mother's whereabouts.

Throughout my childhood, I remember my friends, who were only children like myself, ranting and raving, talking about how much they wanted a little brother or sister to be a part of their families. Someone to play with and confide in, to have a lifelong friend who would always be by their side. They celebrated alongside their families when new babies were announced, bragged to me about the newest member of their families upon the birth of their new siblings, and became annoying little shits who always had their kid brothers and sisters trailing behind them as we grew up with a bustling New York City as our backdrop.

If anything, it all seemed like a huge pain in the ass to me—having to share the small amount of attention my father showed me with another person, someone else to cater to and prance around all while plastering a fake-as-shit smile on my face for my father like I often did with our household staff, all while I silently tormented them when he wasn't paying attention.

Maybe it's because while my name is Saint, I've never felt holy a day in my damn life.

No, instead, I've felt more and more like the dammed devil with each and every passing year.

And I know, without a shadow of a doubt, it's all because of *her*.

Noel Belle came into my life when she was eight years old, nearly half my own age of fourteen.

While I was already a freshman in high school, she was only in third grade when she moved into the Upper East Side brownstone I shared with my father. She was nothing more than a tiny, scrawny little thing with a head full of wild, chestnut curls, and green eyes that took up half her face. We came together unexpectedly when my father—one of the richest businessmen in the US—married her mother—a European actress, who had been filming on location in the city.

Almost immediately, I resented both mother and child—mother for waltzing into my home and rearranging every aspect of my perfectly tailored life after a two-month-long whirlwind romance with my father, and child for putting me in a position where I had to share the small amount of attention I managed to get from the only family I had ever known. We entered into a constant push and pull against one another, almost as if we needed to clash with each other in order to survive.

Through forced family dinners and summer vacations, winter ski trips and milestone celebrations, she tried to become my friend, to get close to me. In return, I tried to push her away by breaking her toys—decapitating her Barbies like they had personally wronged me and smashing every lightbulb for her little Easy Bake Oven she received on our first Christmas as a family before moving to chase away any stupid, little school boy that dared to even look at Noel as she grew from child to teen. I wasn't exactly cruel to her, but I sure as hell wasn't nice either. Using the guise as her hellacious older brother to keep boys as far away from her as possible was fun—almost a sport I succeeded in time and time again.

Deep down inside, though, I knew—even then—that there was something more than just a deep-rooted hatred for her. I just didn't know what the words were for it at the time.

Shortly after Noel turned twelve, I left Manhattan, traveling to California to complete my undergrad degree in finance, hell-bent on making a name for myself without the financial support or clout of my family's last name. The Klaus name had been synonymous with Christmas and toys for generations— hell, it still is. And I was determined to end that streak, wanting nothing to do with the family business that delivered toys directly to Santa's doorstep each year.

Yet time and time again—without fail–the moment I came home for break, we would fall back into our usual pattern of Noel trying to get close while I continued to push her away.

Hastily, I throw shit into my suitcase now as my mind drifts back to the past, and I once again find myself immediately riled up. I think back to the last family holiday we had–a Fourth of July celebration the year she turned sixteen. I came home to visit for the summer after putting in a few final grueling semesters at college, only to find a wide-eyed Noel had transformed. When I left home two years prior, she was my gangly little step-sister, the girl I loved to torment who had a mouth full of metal and thick glasses that were her only defense against her terrible vision. She was always a tad on the nerdy side, but she was still kinda adorable in the way girls are in late nineties teen romances—though I would *never* admit that to another soul.

You know the type I'm talking about: the nerdy-yet-kinda-cute heroine that turns into a perfect ten when she removes her glasses and takes her hair out of the ponytail she's been wearing for years on end after some pathetic jock makes an ill-advised bet with his little fuck-boy friends and takes her to the prom.

Only when I came back, she hadn't just transformed from adorably dorky to hot like some little weird, teenaged movie star.

Oh no, she had turned into a Goddamned knockout.

Gone were the braces and glasses, the acne and awkward leg-to-torso ratio that always made her look like she was a second away from tripping over something invisible. Instead, a near-woman stood in front of me with curves and breasts and long lashes that she batted in my direction while wearing the tiniest fucking bikini she could find.

I knew it was wrong to look at her the way I was; I swear I did.

Still, my body betrayed me.

It was a Thursday evening during the summer, the type of evening where the clothes on my body hung heavy against the humidity in the air. Our doting parents were out celebrating their anniversary over a romantic dinner me and Noel were definitely not invited to. Deciding on a late-night swim to ease the tension in my muscles caused by hours of cross-country travel in tiny airline seats, I stopped short when I noticed the light on in the pool house that sat proudly off the back of our Hamptons summer home. Changing my course, I crossed the pool deck to the door, already annoyed that my stepsister's carelessness had caused me to go out of my way when all I wanted to do was dive into the water warmed by the earlier summer sun and work the kinks from my stiff muscles.

Pushing open the door and expecting to simply flip a switch, I paused when I realized that she hadn't just left the light on. Instead, I found Noel lying on the pull-out couch left for the most hated of overnight guests, the stupid metal bar digging into the back of anyone who dared lay on it for more than a minute. It just went to show you that even with all the money in the world, a pull-out bed is one thing that will *never* be comfortable, no matter the cost.

Her head was lying in the lap of some little jock fuck face no bigger than a toothpick, his hands running through her tangled, wild curls as he locked eyes with me in a move that was a clear challenge. She wore nothing but a damp two-piece, the fabric so scant that she may well have been wearing nothing at all. Her nipples were hard little points beneath the flimsy fabric, her pert little breasts almost on full display. Beer cans littered the table in front of them, and a glassy look in Noel's eyes that I was more than familiar seeing from nights at frat parties had me springing into fast action despite the hatred I always outwardly portrayed toward her.

Yes, she was my annoying little sister that I told myself I couldn't fucking stand. Sure, she made my traitorous body light up brighter than the iconic Rockefeller Center Christmas tree. Still, I wasn't about to turn my back knowing she was about to be taken advantage of while possibly under the influence at the age of sixteen.

I might have been an unscrupulous bastard ninety percent of the time. But even I wasn't a total fucking monster.

With thundering steps, I crossed to where they had been lying, pulled my sister off the clueless boy's lap, and threw an expensive woven blanket at her in one move, watching as she stumbled while trying to catch her footing on the pristine rug that covered much of the pool house's tile floor.

"Wrap yourself in that."

She hesitated, glancing at me with a familiar heat in her eyes that told me a challenge was about to happen. She had given me the look more times than I could count over the years

—almost anytime I tried to genuinely do something nice, she acted like it was the strangest thing in the world. And to her benefit, it wasn't often that I actually did do something to truly benefit her. After a while, I mostly stopped trying, fully leaning into the villainous Scrooge she believed me to be. "Or what? You going to run to Daddy on me, Saint?"

I snapped, everything around me going red as I zoned in on Noel, her chest heaving with anger. Before I could make heads or tails of what I was doing, I had her pressed against the shiplap wall—my body flush against hers, the bare skin of my torso pressed against the almost bare skin of her bikini-clad body. Her sweet, peppermint aroma mixed into the air around us along with the scent of the warm beer she had been drinking. To this day, I can still remember how fucking right it felt to have her curves against the hard planes of my hard chest and toned despite the fact that I knew it was wrong.

So fucking wrong.

She was sixteen.

I was twenty-two.

And she was my fucking stepsister.

"Listen to me, Noel." Behind me, I heard the telltale sound of my stepsister's gentleman caller scampering to leave the pool house, not even bothering to check that the woman who was just lounging in his lap before being unceremoniously pulled from his grasp was okay. But I never turned around to acknowledge him, too caught up in the pull happening between Noel and myself—as if she was trying to lasso me into her very orbit.

The door to the pool house opened and closed, leaving us alone. My anger seethed, ready to boil over the surface. I was pissed at the boy, but even more so, I was pissed at my sister. "Cover yourself up or you're going to get yourself into trouble. Especially with boys like him."

She scoffed, pushing against my chest with her dainty little hands, but I refused to budge, keeping her pinned between me and the wall. "I'm not fucking twelve anymore, Saint. Go ahead. Tell Daddy whatever you want."

"Put. Your fucking. Clothes on. Now," I gritted out between tightly clenched teeth, still closer to her than any brother—blood or otherwise—had the right to be.

"Oh, I see what this is." She gave an appreciative glance over my body, a smug smile curling the sides of her mouth. "This isn't about you wanting to tattle on me, is it, Saint? This is about you wanting me to call *you* Daddy instead, isn't it?"

Goddamn, the words made me hard.

So fucking hard.

But I couldn't, no—I *wouldn't*—act on this.

Fuck, she was my underage kid sister. And sure, we weren't related by blood, but she had been in my life for nearly a decade. I had to get away. Away from her sweet peppermint scent and perky breasts that my hands were itching to reach out and palm.

Without another word, I gently pushed away from her, backing into the open room before I turned and left the pool house, Noel's laughter echoing in the distance as I hurriedly packed my single suitcase and headed to the airport. I knew I could figure out the rest when I got there, but one thing was clear—I couldn't be in the same room with Noel Belle for another second. Hell, if I knew what was good for me, I wouldn't allow myself to ever be in the same state as her ever again.

ONE

Gravel crunches under my tires as the black SUV rental pulls up in front of my home for the next few weeks. While I was told we were meeting at a log cabin in the middle of the forest, I shouldn't be surprised that what sits in front of me now is more of a mini-mansion than the rustic yet quaint log cabin I had in mind.

An enormous stone and log structure sits in front of me, jutting up from the frozen winter's ground like it is as much a part of the landscape as the countless pines that shoot toward the overcast sky. More of a ski chalet than a log cabin, the house sits alone and dark—no neighbors as far as the eye can see, no smoke coming from the multiple chimneys, no twinkling Christmas lights shining from the numerous windows that seem to shoot from the ground to the sky. A thick layer of snow already coats the frozen ground around me, and if the meteorologists are right—which they're usually not—more of the powdery shit people love is on its way.

Cursing the late-night flight that had me landing well after the sun had gone down, my body shivers as I look around, taking in the icy and dark scenery all around me.

Why couldn't my family want to spend the holidays on the fucking beach instead of this frozen hellscape?

Happy that I decided to get here a few days before the rest of the family—and very much looking forward to a few days of peace and quiet before I have to face my sister for the first time since that night in the pool house over two years ago—I pull my oversized duffle from the back seat and head toward the front door.

Punching in the electronic door code my father provided me with, I watch as the light flashes green before I try the handle, push open the door, and walk into a dark, cavernous space. Only when I flip on the light switch and illuminate the otherwise dark entryway, it's immediately clear that I am anything but alone.

Several pairs of women's shoes line the wall, snow melting onto the floor around them into a puddle the size of an ice rink. Winter jackets and soggy sweatshirts hang from nearby hooks, and more pieces of luggage fill the space than I can count. As I look toward the open-concept kitchen, I see numerous bottles of alcohol that look like they have already been opened, the liquid levels at varying heights.

I set my duffle down on a nearby couch and walk further into the house, turning on a few low lights and peeking into rooms as I go. It's still silent, still void of festive, holiday cheer. The only sound comes from my heavy footsteps against the wood floors.

Just as I'm about to call my father to figure out what the hell is going on, laughter rings in the distance, and I turn toward the noise, immediately knowing who the melodic sound belongs to.

Mother fucker.

Long strides quickly eat up the distance, and I'm soon pushing through a door that leads to the rear of the property, ready to tear into my little sister for unknowingly ruining the few fucking days of solitude I had planned.

But I come to a stop when I see the scene in front of me.

In the few minutes it has taken me to walk through the house, the snow has begun to fall again. Big, fat flakes rain down from the sky, illuminated by the twinkling fairy lights that are wrapped around the pergola that covers the entire expanse of the outdoor patio.

A hot tub is tucked into the far corner of the space, steam wafting into the cold, night air from its surface while gentle, classical Christmas music plays from nearby speakers designed to look like rocks that are part of the natural landscape. In the middle of the hot tub, Noel sits, a serene smile on her face, her head tipped up toward the heavens as the snow cascades around her.

Like a magical, holiday sprite, her button nose crinkles when a flake lands on its tip, yet her smile never falters, and her eyes never open.

Christ, is it possible she's gotten even more beautiful in the last two years since I've been away?

Like the sick fuck I am, I stand off to the side and continue to watch her as she sits, unaware of my presence.

The end of her curls touch the water before clinging to the soft skin of her shoulders. She moves her hands through the hot water as if reveling in the feel of it against her body. Delicate snowflakes land against her ridiculously long lashes before quickly melting away without a trace of their short-lived existence.

Stepping back further into the shadows when I hear a door open from across the expansive patio, I'm ready for a fight, fully expecting her to have brought some little college-aged fuck up to rub in my face.

But instead, I watch as another woman walks toward the hot tub, a glass of champagne in hand, a red satin robe her only protection against the night's chill. The unknown woman crosses the patio, her wavy black hair hanging loosely almost to the top of her ass.

When she reaches the hot tub, her back toward me, she drops the robe to the ground, and I almost groan at the sight.

Her body is free from clothing, a deliciously perky ass pointed in my direction that I immediately think about sinking my teeth into. Unlike my sister, who is all flawless, creamy, pale skin unmarked from ink, this woman is all tattoos. Running up and down both arms and legs, I can't make out the designs from this distance, but I can tell that they're hot as fuck. From my position in the shadows, I can see they cover most of her back as well, and if I squint my eyes just a bit, I think I can see one trailing up the side of her neck.

I know I should announce my presence, that I should give this stranger the opportunity to shield herself from my hungry gaze. Instead, I stand rooted to the spot, watching as she gracefully climbs into the hot tub alongside my stepsister.

She moves through the water with ease, the bubbles from the jacuzzi jets tickling her skin as she grows closer and closer to my sister. I keep waiting for her to stop, expecting her to claim a nearby seat and begin a conversation. For the two to acknowledge one another.

But oh, no.

Instead, she walks confidently through the water and up to Noel, who still sits with a gentle smile on her serene face. Then, the unknown woman climbs onto my sister's lap, straddling Noel where she sits with her back against the hard, plastic side of the hot tub.

What the fuck?

Leave now, I tell myself. *Take your perverted fucking mind with your rock-hard dick back inside the house, and get the idea of a naked woman pushing her flawless body up against your little sister out of your goddammed mind.*

Yeah, it's what I tell myself. But again, I refuse to listen to the rational part of my brain. Instead, I inch cautiously closer to the pair, groaning as my dick brushes up against my pants, while thankful for the sounds of the jacuzzi for keeping me hidden from their eyes. I'm a dirty, perverted sex ninja hell-bent on fulfilling my rawest, voyeuristic fantasies that I've never dared to share with anyone.

My sister smiles at the woman, her plump lips parting at whatever was said before her entire head falls back and laughter fills the otherwise silent night.

Noel's arms come out of the water, linking around the woman's neck, before she surges up and kisses the mystery guest.

My brain is on overload, trying to make heads or tails of the situation unfolding around me like some late-night version of my favorite skin-a-max porn that I stumbled upon as a teen who spent way too much time with his right hand.

First, no one is supposed to be here for the next two days. This is supposed to be my quiet serenity before the madness of a Klaus-Belle family fucking Christmas. This is the time I carved out in my extremely busy schedule for myself. I'm supposed to be the one sitting in that fucking hot tub—a cigar in one hand, a glass of whiskey in the other—as the snow comes down around me. And yeah, I know that makes me sound like some ungrateful, entitled, spoiled little shit, but whatever—I was looking forward to it.

Secondly, my stepsister—the boy-crazy, wanna-be society girl who loves to parade around in front of the paparazzi while spending Mommy and Daddy's money—is kissing another woman. And not just kissing her like some random drunk-girl dare that sorority girls live for. No, she is kissing her like she means it. With a passion that I have yet to experience for myself despite being six years older than her.

Don't get me wrong, I get plenty of pussy. I fuck whenever I want and with whomever I want. But it's just that—fucking. What these two women are doing in front of my eyes? Hell, their lips are locked in what can only be described as an erotic tango as they each take turns fighting for dominance against one another's mouths.

The last thing my mind catches on—and so help me God, why am I only noticing it now—is that not only is the mystery woman naked, but so is my sister. Under the gentle twinkling lights, her skin radiates a golden hue, almost as if backlighting an angel with a golden halo atop her head. But I know now, that lighting aside, she's just as much the devil as I am.

Noel writhes against the other woman's body, as if needing to feel more. As if all her pleasure is held in the hands of this mystery woman with the gorgeous ass and inked skin and long, black hair that I want to wrap around my fist and tug—hard.

Desperately trying, I fail to pull my gaze from the pair, unaware that their seductive dance is on full display to another's eyes. I'm salivating like the fucking big, bad wolf about to devour his prey as I sweep my gaze up and down their bodies. I watch as my sister runs her hands up the other woman's back, how their flesh slides against one another from the wetness of the water. I listen to their captivating noises—low moans and small gasps that can barely be heard over the sounds of the hot tub. I grow increasingly hard until my cock is achingly painful behind the zipper of my black dress slacks.

The song on the speaker changes, a bizarrely creepy rendition of Jingle Bells, that has me hitting pause of the real-life porn unfolding in front of my eyes. Slowly, I back further into the shadows, retracing my steps until I'm no longer within distance to watch the gratuitous erotica in front of me.

Once back in the house, I grab my duffle before tossing it into the nearest bedroom. Then, I head back to the SUV to retrieve the rest of my luggage. All the while, I try—and fail—to get the act I just witnessed out of my mind.

Placing the luggage in the bedroom, I return to the kitchen and take a seat at the built-in island. I grab the nearest bottle of liquor, pour with a heavy hand into one of the glasses from atop the granite countertop, and wait for my sister and the mystery woman to reappear from the cold night, where the only thing they were together was blistering fucking hot.

TWO

Feminine giggles bounce off the hallway walls before the two women stumble their way into the kitchen where I sit stoically at the island. Now wearing matching red satin robes, Noel's back is to me, her companion guiding her with hands rooted firmly on my sister's hips. Between stolen kisses and quiet moans, they whisper words to one another that I can't overhear. It's a contrast to see them both in such little fabric while I still wear the layers I wore earlier while on the plane.

The woman stops abruptly when she enters the huge kitchen, bringing my sister to a halt alongside her. Wide, blue eyes meet my own, surprise lighting up her features as she struggles with finding a stranger in the kitchen in what is meant to be a quiet, abandoned house.

Sensing the change in mood, that the playfulness of her companion has quickly evaporated, my sister looks at the woman before following her line of sight. Her eyes turn from playful to angry in an instant when she sets her own green eyes on me.

"What the fuck are you doing here, Saint? No one is supposed to be here until Friday!" she asks, her voice holding just the barest hint of a British accent left over from her days living overseas as a child. She tries to hide it, to conceal it from the world, yet it always seems to sneak out when she's angry.

And if there is one thing I love in this life, it's making my stepsister mad.

I give her body a slow once over—fully appreciating just what a gorgeous woman she has turned into. "I presume that I could ask the same of you, my darling sister. Aren't you going to introduce me to your friend?"

I try to appear unfazed, casually sipping on the whiskey that has been warming my glass as I waited for them to return from their hot tub playtime I found myself so desperately wanting to be a part of.

The indignant little brat rolls her eyes at me. "Not that it is any of *your* business, *darling brother*," she spits the words with such vehemence, it's a surprise venom doesn't drip from her tongue, "but this is my girlfriend, Holly."

"Ah, I see how it is." I wiggle my eyebrows at her suggestively. "Finally realized those little pimply college boys would never be able to give you what you were looking for, so you decided to switch teams thinking a woman would know your body better than any man ever could?"

I know I deserve it, but I'm still not expecting the sting of her palm as it meets my cheek. "Again, not that it is any of *your* business," she punctuates the words with a short, red fingernail poking me in the chest, "but I've known I was queer since I was nine years old—that I found both women and men attractive. Maybe you would have known that had you taken the time to get to know me and not always ran away the second things got uncomfortable, if you had stood up to me and fought instead of scurrying away like a scared, little bunny rabbit."

Ouch, that might have hurt worse than the slap across my face.

And I hate to admit it, but she's not exactly lying. I did run away from her—and I did so often. But I did it to protect what would have inevitably happened if I stayed in New York. I did it to protect myself. To protect her. And never has that been as apparent as it is right now. I can pretend to hate her all I want. Pretend that she's always been nothing but my pain in the ass little sister who was always in my way.

But that isn't exactly the total truth.

And maybe it isn't Noel's complete truth either.

The signs feel almost obvious now—her constant need to be as close to me as possible, the suggestive glances and the outrageous way she paraded herself around our parent's house half-naked as she blossomed into womanhood. Could it be that the entire time she was trying to get closer to me, she was actually trying to show her interest in a way that only an inexperienced teen could do?

Not that I have time to dissect that fucking bombshell of a revelation right now.

In her anger, she hasn't noticed that her robe is hanging wide open. The gentle slope of her breasts—dangerously close to being fully exposed—taunt me, her creamy stomach begs me to trace its smooth expanse with my tongue. Between her thighs, I can make out the tiniest patch of curls before dark shadows take over. Suddenly, I find myself cursing the dim lights that provide only the barest bit of illumination inside this monstrous and otherwise dark cabin.

Get a hold of yourself, Saint.

You cannot go there.

"You have to leave," Noel tells me flatly. Thankfully, it distracts me from the thoughts of pushing her against the island, of spreading her out on top of the cold granite before leaning over her body to lick her cunt while her skin pebbles from the dichotomy of sensations.

I snort in response. "The fuck I do. I did my due diligence, made sure that no one would be here. As far as I'm concerned, you and your little girlfriend can gladly leave. Give me the peace and fucking quiet I know I'm not going to have with you here."

She laughs in my face.

The fucking audacity.

"Little Saint Nick, not getting his way and pouting about it– as always. What's wrong, brother? Are you afraid to be alone in a house with two grown women who love to explore each other's bodies? Are you worried that you're going to hear us fucking and get turned on. Just like you did two years ago when I called you Daddy?"

Pushing up from the barstool I've patiently been perched on, I step closer to my stepsister. "Forgive me for wanting a silent fucking night, Noel. Not that you would ever understand the concept of silence."

I step closer to her as she huffs out her frustration. One, two, three steps until I'm so close that she has to crane her neck to meet my eyes. All the while, I feel Holly's big, blue eyes bouncing between us as if she's torn between watching the scene play out and intervening.

If my sister thinks I'm going to back up, that I'm going to turn and run like I have so many times before, she is sorely mistaken. Instead, I trail my fingertips up and over her exposed stomach, silently loving the way she sucks in a gasp as my fingers touch her skin. "But then again, as much as I do love silence, I also love the sound of a woman as she comes. And we both know from your past performances that you are sure to be a *fantastic* actress."

Continuing to taunt her with my fingertips, I lightly travel upward over the concave place between her breasts. Up, up, up, I travel, tracing the column of her neck before gently wrapping my fingers around her throat. Her eyes go wide, yet I don't move. I don't squeeze or apply pressure, simply hold her in place, my eyes boring into her soul with a fierceness I've never felt before. "Tell me, Sweetheart. Does she make you come so hard that you see fucking stars? Does she make you climax so hard that your legs are unsteady, and your entire body shakes afterward? Because if so, it might be worth it to stay just to listen to you come from behind a closed door somewhere in this lodge."

Her eyes darken, a deep, forest green with rings of jade at the outermost edge that work to hypnotize me. "Who said anything about it being behind closed doors? We came early so we could use the space. Don't expect me to change my plans on account of you being here. Maybe if you're on the nice list this year, we'll let you watch."

Evil little fucking temptress. She should have been named after the devil himself.

I drop my hand from around her neck, flicking the fabric of her robe, which still hangs open around her body. "Stay out of my way and I'll stay out of yours."

Picking up my glass, I start to exit the kitchen but turn around quickly, swiping the expensive bottle of whiskey from the counter as I retreat to my room in haste.

And as I go, I hear their laughter echoing behind me the entire fucking way, just like the last time I ran away from the siren that is my stepsister.

THREE

Of all the modern amenities this place seems to have, I was surprised to see an old, digital alarm clock perched atop the nightstand in the room I sent myself to for my self-imposed solitary confinement. One of those small, black boxes with red numbers, a few switches, and a large, flat snooze button, it would be more at home in a cheap, roadside motel than a swanky, palatial winter retreat tucked remotely in the woods.

And now, after nearly five hours of staring at the numbers on that dammed alarm as minute after minute ticked by with near-glacial speed while laughter poured from the living space of the house, I've had enough.

There will be no sugar plums dancing in my head tonight. Only visions of my own personal vixen—not to be confused with Santa's helpful reindeer of the same name.

I crack open the door to my bedroom, exhaling when I don't hear any sound coming from the common areas of the house. It's been nearly an hour since I've heard the voices and giggles of my stepsister and Holly, and at nearly four in the morning, I'm thankful I seem to finally be in the clear. Of that, my mind and still impossibly hard cock seem to be in agreement.

Still, I'm quiet upon approach.

The living room, which previously stood bare, is now covered in Christmas decorations as if Santa's elves descended from the North Pole to cast magic over the cabin. A large tree stands proudly in the middle of the room, wrapped in no less than a million twinkling lights and just as many ornate, glass ornaments in every color of the rainbow. From atop the tree, an angel in shades of whites, creams, and silvers holds a candle in each hand as if beckoning onlookers to admire the tree's beauty.

My eyes don't stop at the tree. They take in the faux pine garland and lights that wrap around a railing on the second floor and the multiple figurines of Santa and his helpers that have appeared as if out of thin air. Turning to the opposite side of the room, my gaze sweeps over the fireplace mantel where five stockings hang, neatly spaced in the same colors as the tree's baubles.

Mom, Dad, Saint, Noel, Holly.

Each name is embroidered in bright white thread, complimenting the patchwork of random fabrics that make up each stocking. As if the names Saint and Noel weren't bad enough on their own, now we've thrown another ridiculous nod to the Christmas season into the fucking mix.

Staring at the stockings, my mind begins to drift once again. Not for the first time since I learned of the relationship between Noel and Holly just several hours ago, I find myself wondering how long the two women have been an item as I continue my slow perusal of the decor that has transformed the space from something cold and sterile to something warm and welcoming. It's different from the many Christmases of our family's past, where every knickknack and strand of lights was put in the perfect position by a company hired to trim our trees and deck our halls. There were no macaroni-covered ornaments, handmade by tiny hands in school. No uneven clumps of tinsel hanging from wilting pine branches after hours spent finding the perfect tree, and no time spent with one another as we hung ornaments while watching stop-motion cheesy yet classic Christmas movies. Hell, until I was nearly twenty, I never even knew that *Die Hard* was a Christmas movie. Instead, it was fancy cocktail parties and charity galas that Noel and I were often left out of, being shipped to our grandparents for long weekends or turned over to the hired help.

Not to say we were neglected by our parents—because we certainly weren't. Hell, to this day, neither my sister nor myself have wanted for anything materialistic, and I know we're extremely lucky for that. There were simply certain times of the year and certain events where it was expected that children would be seen and not heard. With as volatile a relationship as Noel and I had, our parents found it was easier for us to not be seen *or* heard.

I stare out the large, floor-to-ceiling windows that line one wall of the living room, watching as snow continues to fall from the heavens above with no signs of slowing down. Despite the lack of natural and artificial light coming from outside, the inches of snow reflect the moonlight, allowing me to see as far as the edge of the forest that surrounds the property.

As I stand and watch the peaceful sight, I contemplate how different this year already is from the years past—another person added to our often-fraught family gatherings. But even more than my thoughts on how this year will continue to be different, I wonder how Noel and Holly met—if this is the first time they have spent a holiday together, if my parents have met Holly before, and how they reacted to my sister coming out to them. I rack my brain, wondering why I spent years pushing my sister away, when maybe I needed the warmth she so freely gave to everyone but me, and fear it is too late to receive the same warmth now.

And perhaps more sinisterly, I wonder what the two lovers look like when they are in bed together, their hot, sweaty bodies rubbing against each other like they did in the jacuzzi mere hours ago.

"Hey there."

The raspy voice startles me from my thoughts, and I turn to find Holly watching me with curious, blue eyes. I approach, equal parts cautious and speculative myself, crossing from the living room and entering into the kitchen where Holly stands, a mug of steaming liquid in one hand, a bottle of water in the other. Sans robe, she now wears a pair of short red shorts that are tiny enough for her ass cheeks to hang out of the back and a matching tank that barely covers her midriff. Fuzzy, white fur lines the bottom of the shorts and tank, making her look like a naughty little wet dream of an elf. I consciously stop myself from reaching out to trail my finger across the soft fur. Instead, I drop my hand to my side, the digits curling into a fist in some ill attempt at self-perseverance as I take in the matching Santa hat that sits atop her rumpled hair. It shouldn't make her look even sexier, yet somehow it does.

"After all this time, I finally get to meet the illustrious Saint Klaus." Her voice is far raspier than I expect. A little rough around the edges just as she appears to be with her tattoos and long, tangled hair. I can't quite tell if her knotted hair and husky voice are intentional or if it is a result of romping between the sheets—and between the legs of Noel—but I find myself desperate to know the answer. Desperate for more fodder for the late-night fantasies that plague my brain when I'm searching for sleep that never comes. Surely, when I think of Noel in the future—because let's face it, I think of her often, even if it pains me to admit it—I'll also be picturing this smoke show of a woman next to her.

Or on top of her...

"The one person who stands between me and the full heart of the woman I love. I have to say, the pictures I've seen really don't do you justice. But then again, that might be due to the barely-clothed women constantly hanging all over you in every single paparazzi picture that tries to steal the focus of the camera lens."

Christ, if this is how she acts all the time, she's perfect for Noel. Two beautiful, bratty women desperately in need of a firm hand on the backside in order to curb their less-than acceptable behavior.

Not wanting to deal with her snark on top of what I've already been subjected to this evening, I turn, expecting to make a quick retreat back to the small room I've been boarded up in all night. Hell, if I have to stay locked away in that room until the near year—away from those two temptresses—so fucking be it.

But Holly's words stop me in my tracks. "Amazingly enough, every single one of those women resembled your darling little stepsister in at least one way. One week, Noel would be in the tabloids in a pink dress. A few days later and you'd be out with a lookalike—in appearance and fashion. Another time, she'd show up to an event wearing a structured black suit. What's on *Page Six* the following week? Illustrious playboy Saint Klaus, another stunner on his arm—this time in a structured black suit. I truly am surprised that no one ever caught on."

"Caught on to what?" I ask, my teeth clenched so tightly at her insinuation that I'm surprised I don't chip a tooth.

At her silence, I slowly turn toward her and watch as she flashes me a saccharine sweet smile—as if she's an innocent little girl trying to get out of trouble. But her words are anything but sweet and innocent. "Caught on to the fact that you're just as hot for your stepsister as she is for you. Tell me, did you play dress-up with your dates? Use them as your very own fantasy fuck-doll? How many times have you accidentally called out her name as you spilled into some random woman's cunt? Hope you made them all sign NDAs before getting down and dirty."

I shake my head, trying to desperately comprehend what she is saying—trying to deny the very idea that I only began to accept the moment I saw Noel sitting with her perfectly angelic face tilted up to the sky in the hot tub.

That I desperately want my stepsister.

But I'll be dammed if I admit that to this woman—a near fucking stranger. Sure, she's gorgeous, but her long legs and slim waist don't make her any less dangerous. On the contrary, they make her downright menacing.

If word ever got out that I was attracted to the woman who I grew up next to—that I want to do unspeakable things to her naked body...*fuck*. It would kill my father's business. The largest supplier of toys that delivers directly to the North Pole cannot succeed if its entire business model is based on a family scandal. As far as our parents are concerned, as far as society is concerned, we're as good as blood-related. Saint and Noel, heir and heiress to the Klaus Toy fortune—not that either of us wants what's ours.

"You have no idea what you're talking about," I tell her with a forced laugh, directing my full attention back to the bombshell standing in front of me. For a moment, I imagine what it would be like had we met under different circumstances. Clearly, she has a bratty side, and it's a side I wouldn't mind trying my hand at taming.

Holly walks closer to me, eating up the space between us without trepidation. She's bold, just as bold as my sister. With mere inches between us, she holds my gaze, challenging me to look away first with her bright, blue eyes that remind me of a crystalline sky after a frigid, winter snowstorm. They sparkle with mischief, as if already knowing whatever comes from their owner's mouth next will likely push me closer to an edge that I know there is no coming back from.

"Sometimes," she skirts a hand up my chest, covered now only by a thin, long-sleeved cotton Henley, "she calls out your name when she's asleep."

My spine goes rigid, and I'm unable to speak. There is no witty retort, no quick comeback to reply with. Instead, I stand stock still, the thought of my sister calling out to me in her sleep driving a chisel deep into the middle of my stone-cold heart.

Holly continues before I can protest. Her fingers continue to trail upward until she wraps her hand around the back of my neck. "At first, I thought it was because you did something that scared her. That she was trying to escape some sick and twisted torture you subjected her to as a child." Her free hand comes down to palm my cock through my loose sleep pants. She wraps her fingers around my length and squeezes—hard enough that I let out a hiss through my tightly clenched teeth. "When I thought you had hurt her, that you scared such a beautiful, pure woman—well, I wanted to tear your dick off and shove it up your own ass." Her grip loosens, but she doesn't let me go. "But then, one night, I really listened as she said your name, and I finally realized that she wasn't saying Saint because she was trying to escape you. She wasn't even saying your name at all. She was *moaning* it."

My cock jerks, and the smirk Holly throws my way proves she felt it, too.

"And here's the thing, Saint. I must be more of a masochist than I originally thought I was because I want to give your sister everything she wants—even if that thing is you."

I can't figure out her angle, and it's starting to piss me off.

"What are you getting at?" I snap.

Holly presses up onto her tiptoes, her lips centimeters away from my ear. "I'm saying that I'm getting ready to go wake up Sleeping Beauty. That I'm going to bring her out to the living room, light a fire in that enormous fireplace, spread her out on that bearskin rug, which I sincerely hope is faux fur, and devour every fucking inch of her body. And to the contrary of what you might believe, I'm *very* open to sharing."

I narrow my eyes at her, still not completely sure of what she is suggesting.

With both of her hands now wrapped around my neck, her body flush against mine, Holly kisses my jaw. She kisses my neck and my cheek before placing one last kiss against my lips. "I'm saying—*Saint*—that being on the naughty list is way more fun than the alternative. What's stopping you?"

And with that final word still on her lips, she pushes away from me, picking up both the long-forgotten mug and bottle of water before sauntering up to the second floor of the cabin as if she doesn't have a care in the world and hasn't just left my mind —and dick—a straining, dripping fucking mess.

FOUR

The words ring through my head on repeat as I fight with the angel and devil sitting on my shoulders. I'm sitting on the edge of a double bed that is way too tiny for a man of my stature. My head in my hands, I teeter back and forth again and again, wondering if what Holly was propositioning me with was true or some cruel joke used to lure me into some wicked trap more suited for the likes of Old Hallow's Eve than Christmas.

"I'm saying—Saint—that being on the naughty list is way more fun than the alternative. What's stopping you?"

And for fuck's sake, I have been nice. As far as I'm concerned, I've been nice for way too fucking long when all I've really wanted to do is stake my claim on the bratty, little step-sister who made the last decade of my life a living fucking hell. When all I wanted to do was spank her naughty, perfect, upside-down heart of an ass with each boy she paraded in front of me. Wanted to tear what minimal clothes she wore off her body so I could greedily drink in her perfectly petite body with curves in *all* the right places.

Instead, I walked away from her time and time again.

Instead, I ran when she challenged me.

Instead, I pushed her away when the entire fucking time, I should have been pulling her closer.

Instead...instead...instead.

Well, you know what?

Fuck instead.

With my security bottle of booze firmly clutched in hand, I open the door of the bedroom, unaware of what waits on the other side. My bare feet quietly plod against the cold, wooden floor, and when I come to the end of the hallway, I stop short, in awe of the sight unfolding in front of me.

From the dark shadows of the hallway, I watch entrancedly

as Holly sinks to the cold, hardwood floor in front of my stepsister. She pushes her oversized nightshirt up to expose her perfect fucking breasts—barely more than a handful—forcing what amounts to a scrap of fabric into Noel's hands before placing a gentle kiss against her flat stomach.

Despite the low light flickering across the walls from the living room fireplace, I can see the gooseflesh as it breaks out across her skin, and it makes my already uncomfortable dick almost unbearable. With one hand still on my glass bottle of whiskey, I palm myself over my sweatpants with the other, giving myself a hard squeeze to try to control the overwhelming urge to stride into the room and claim both of these women as my own.

Noel whimpers as her lover drags her panties down her legs, and I swear to Christ, I almost explode in my fucking pants like an inexperienced teenager who just got his hands on his dad's hidden porn stash.

It's a needy yet quiet little mewl, the sound that escapes into the otherwise quiet night barely audible over the sound of the low music playing over the surround sound and the crackling fire coming from the large, brick fireplace that stands in the middle of the room. It's a sound I've obsessed about drawing from her pillowy soft lips since before it was ever appropriate to think about her in a sexual way.

Though truly, is it ever appropriate to think about one's own stepsister's plump lips that could likely suck the chrome off a fucking doorknob?

A moan across the room brings me back to the present, where Holly's fingers trace a teasing pathway over Noel's thighs, growing closer and closer to her cunt with each and every pass of her fingertips. Despite the distance between us—me hidden in the shadows of the hallway like some perverted Krampus who has come to scare children and steal Christmas while Noel stands wanton as delicate fingers circle closer and closer to her center—I swear I can smell her arousal.

It drives me absolutely feral, and a low growl escapes from somewhere deep inside me. A dank, dark cavern where I keep all my most taboo desires locked away.

Like the absolute white-hot need I now feel to punish my stepsister for the relentless teasing over the years. The need I feel to pull her over my lap and redden those perfect heart-shaped ass cheeks that I long to sink my teeth into as her girl-friend watches on, waiting for her own turn under my heavy palm for the evil part she has played in seducing me with this wicked display of spank bank material.

Before I can stop myself or think better of it, I emerge from the shadows like a villainous underlord, slowly and deliber-ately crossing the living room, my eyes trained on the two women the entire time.

My sister's eyes meet mine as I stride across the room, coming to stand mere inches away from where she is pressed with her back against the nearby wall. Holly's hands stop their careful movements, stilling her exploration of the creamy expanse of skin in front of us.

"Tell me, my darling little sister." I reach out and grasp Holly's hand in mine, placing it back on Noel's smooth body that I long to touch without the barrier between us. "Have I truly been blind this entire time?"

While my voice and hands are firm and steady, I'm secretly ready to combust on the inside, swearing I can feel the heat of my sister's hot skin through the hand of her lover.

Using Holly's hand as a guide, we slide across my stepsister's skin in tandem. Across her stomach, over her thighs, we move closer and closer until the only barrier between the sweetest cunt I've ever smelled is another woman's hand.

I feel Noel as she pushes against both Holly's hand and my own. Searching for more pressure that I deny her with great satisfaction. "Could I have been touching your body this entire time? Been tasting that sweet, sweet pussy of yours since the day you turned eighteen?"

"I've always been yours, Saint."

Noel's eyes stay locked on mine in a silent dare. It's a dare for me to let go of the last shred of restraint that is holding me back. A dare to give her what she has silently been asking of me since before I ever recognized the signs.

I'm so close to breaking down, to throwing caution to the wind. Then, without warning, the decision is made for me. The hand between me and Noel is gone, and every one of my fucking depraved fantasies is coming to life in front of my eyes.

Instantly, my fingers are coated in her slick, wet heat, and I have to stop myself from immediately lifting them to my mouth to have a taste of what I know will be the most delicious delicacy known to man.

I know it's wrong—know that while she has apparently wanted me since she was just a young, naive teenager—she hasn't given me consent to touch her in such an intimate way. I know that I should pull away, that we should talk without the audience of her lover, yet I can't bring myself to move my hand from between her creamy thighs.

Before I can pull my head out of my ass long enough to

know what is happening, Holly is behind me, pressing me closer and closer to Noel. She pants in my ear as her body writhes against my back, grinding up against me like a feral cat in heat. "She's so fucking wet, isn't she?"

"Soaked," I say, my brain still working overtime to comprehend that my hands are on my stepsister's body. That another woman—her *lover*—is pressed so tightly to my body that a single fucking hair wouldn't fit into the space between us.

I can't even stop to contemplate how wrong it is. I can't stop to worry about the toy company or what my dad and stepmother will say if they ever find out about this. I can't bother to think about the repercussions of my actions because, in this moment, I have the woman I have always wanted under my hands, another gorgeous goddess pressed against my back with her gentle curves and tight nipples—both women willing and ready for the taking.

And all of it feels so *right*.

Nails gently rake up and down my back, Holly playfully teasing me with those red talons that are slightly longer than my sister's own nails. "Look up, Saint."

Doing as she says, I let out a low, menacing chuckle when I see the sprig of mistletoe hanging above us by equally-as-festive red, velvet ribbon.

"Go ahead," Holly says. "Give your beautiful little sister a kiss."

Again, I follow her instructions as if she has cast a spell over my body. My lips crash against Noel's with a force great enough to knock the world off its axis. She whimpers into my mouth as I part her lips with my tongue, and my cock weeps in my pants, desperate for touch or pressure or *any* kind of relief from the maddening hardness that has been happening for hours on end. My hands leave her body to tangle in her curls, tugging at the strands with just the slightest amount of pressure.

Finally, I pull back, searching Noel's beautiful green eyes

with my own. My words come out with a bite, and I immediately regret it when her eyes dim. "Is this what you want? Was this at the top of your Christmas wish list this year?"

Her hands come up to rest on my chest, and it's the first time I'm overwhelmed with the sensation of four hands on my body at once as opposed to two.

I've done my fair amount of sharing over the years, always in the context of sharing another woman with a friend and never as it is at this moment. It's a powerful feeling, multiple partners with their hands on me. Nails still teasing my back through the thin fabric of my shirt, both Holly and I wait, aware that at any moment, everything could come crashing to a stop with Noel's simple words.

As my stepsister speaks, her voice trembles. And it's at this moment that I know she's not playing. That this isn't some cruel joke she and Holly concocted to torment me. In fact, her voice is so strained, it's as if she's holding back tears, and it sends another small piece of the brick wall around my heart careening to the floor. "It's been at the top of every list since I knew what want and need were. Since I knew what sex was, since I knew what passion and control were. Since I knew what *kink* was. I might be young, and I might love Holly, but that doesn't stop me from wanting to know what you feel like inside of me—from *needing* to know what you feel like inside of me."

With wide eyes, I continue to stare at her as she continues. "I know what you like to do, Saint. I've seen the women you've been with and know what you're known for within your circle of friends. And if I can have it for even one day, have the two people who hold my entire heart in their hands, then who am I to turn that away?"

Reaching out, I cup her jaw in my hand, the smoothness of her skin sending a chill over my body. I close my eyes for a moment, relishing in the feel of her smooth skin against my rough palm. "You know this will change everything between us."

She scoffs, more like the bratty little sister I've been secretly fond of for years and less like the wanton woman sharing her deepest desires from just mere moments before. "Saint, we've never had *anything* between us, so how could *everything* possibly change?"

I raise a brow, not in question, but in slight agreement. "And your mom and my dad? They can absolutely never find out. Noone can ever know about this. It would kill my dad's business."

Noel gives me a slight nod, though I can tell she doesn't quite agree. "We're not actually related, Saint."

"I know that!" I say, louder than expected.

I try to back up, to put some space between myself and Noel as I once again seem to slip back into old thought patterns, but the body behind me stops me in my place.

"Look at her," a voice says from behind me. "Don't run away from her again, Saint. Can't you see how badly she wants you? How badly she *aches* for you?"

How the hell I managed to forget there was another person —another *woman*—in the room, I'll never understand. But for a minute, it was just me and Noel, no other woman pressed against my back, no third person to complicate an already tangled mess.

Holly continues, her voice soft and calm, like someone trying to capture the attention of a skittish animal. Never thought I'd be the skittish one, but here we are. "Doesn't she deserve to have everything she's ever wanted? Don't you deserve the same? From where I'm standing, we're three consenting adults. What's wrong with having a little extra Christmas cheer while we can?"

"And what about the relationship between the two of you?

How do you know that this won't fuck things up for the both of you?"

Hell, if I'm going to give into this sinful temptation, I need to know that Noel is confident in her decision. Because there is simply no way that I can keep her for myself. As tempting as the idea suddenly seems, this isn't about forever. This is about one day of giving into our most basic desires before handing her fully back over and into the capable hands of her lover.

My stepsister turns her nose up at me in an act of clear defiance. "As sweet as it is that you're worried about my well-being, can we just agree that I'm an adult and that I'm capable of making my own decisions? And my decision is that I want you *and* Holly together—for one day."

"That's all I can give you."

"That's all I'm asking for," she replies.

I sigh, seriously contemplating my decision despite the fact that two half-naked women have already had their bodies pressed against mine for the last few minutes.

"We do things *my* way," I address both women, first looking at Noel before craning my neck to lock eyes with Holly. "That means we sit down and discuss things first—like the three adults we all keep claiming to be. We talk about limits and expectations, about wants and needs."

Holly snorts behind me. "Sounds sexy."

Turning my head back to her, I glare. "Negotiations can be sexy as hell—you'll see."

"Negotiations?" Noel says. "This is starting to sound more like a fucking business deal than you helping to fulfill one of my life-long fantasies."

"Have you already forgotten, baby girl? Weren't you the one just telling me minutes ago that you knew all about your big brother? That you knew how he liked to play and tease? I'm starting to think that maybe you don't know as much about me as you first thought you did."

Noel and Holly share one of those private glances that I'm not privy to, but it doesn't anger me that they are sharing a moment that I'm not a part of. Instead, I appreciate that they are seemingly speaking to one another, checking in and assessing the situation much like I would with any other play partner in any other scenario.

Finally, Noel breaks the silence, her voice smoothing over me from where she still stands behind me. "Okay, we'll play by your rules."

And that—those six words—are enough to have my mind concocting all sorts of sexy plans for the hours still to come.

FIVE

A few long hours later, the two women meet me back in the large, open kitchen—the place where we first came together with the force of waves crashing upon the shore, when they stumbled into the room after their hot tub tryst.

If the sun were shining, I think it would be high in the sky by this time of day, but with the snow that has yet to stop falling, I can barely make out the fiery orb as it soars over ninety million miles away.

While I was certainly eager to begin our one night of forbidden passion the second the subject was broached, I knew I needed to enter this with a clear and even head—*and* temper —or that everything could quickly turn to shit.

Hell, it still possibly could when the two women get a look at what Saint Klaus is *really* about.

After a quick nap and a *very* cold shower that did nothing to help my aching balls, I scoured the rental for anything that could serve a dual purpose—not only in whatever its true use was but for anything that could also be used as an implement I would normally use on any of the women I casually play with at the numerous specialized clubs and lounges custom built for those with tastes like mine.

Now, as the two women stare at the various items I've scrounged up from around the house, I can't help the somewhat sinister smile that curls the corners of my mouth upward despite knowing that I've vowed to take it easy on both of them.

Holly picks up a scarf, the thick, knitted material running through her fingers before she puts it back in its place and moves to a flat hairbrush I found sitting on a bathroom counter on the opposite side of the house. Probably left over from some other rich family who came for a good, old-fashioned getaway, I bet whoever owned it never thought of it being used as a spanking tool on a grown-ass adult.

My stepsister moves with more trepidation than Holly, her eyes widening as they take in a large roll of cling wrap, a spatula, a wooden spoon, and a tub of coconut oil. I don't plan on using all of it, but I want her to think I am—want her to expect the unexpected when it comes to what I might do to her once I finally have her beneath my hands.

Noel's fingers lightly graze one of several strands of Christmas garland, before she continues her perusal of the items laid out in front of her. "You...you're going to use all of this on me?" Her voice is barely above a whisper, and while she puts on a brave face, I can tell she is uncomfortable by the sight of the zip ties, leather belt, and clothespins scattered about the table.

I cross to where she stands at the large, wooden table, Holly still at her side. With a gentle hand, I brush a few strands of her hair behind her ear, feeling more and more confident with each and every passing second that this night will be one none of us will ever forget. I'm in control, I remind myself. This is no different than any of the other times I've scened with any of the other women I've taken to bed. "I'm going to give you everything you can handle, sweetheart. And when you think you've had enough, that you're at your limit—I'm going to push you even further. Until you break beneath my hands."

While her face remains impassive, I don't miss the slight tremor that works its way through her body at my words. She's a scared little mouse, and I'm the big, bad lion that could overwhelm her with a simple swipe of a giant paw. "But first, I'm going to show you how each and every item on this table works —how it will feel against your skin, so you know what to expect." I turn to look at my sister's lover, capturing her gaze with mine. Her blue eyes shimmer, her brows arched high on her face, and from the excitement in her eyes, I come to the foregone conclusion that she is the more experienced of the two women. "And Holly is going to help me, aren't you?"

Holly eagerly nods in assent, almost urging me on with body language alone.

It's the first time I've managed to fully appreciate her beauty. Of course, I noticed she was gorgeous the second I laid eyes on her, watching as that sinfully thin robe she was wearing floated to the concrete patio floor around her body like a billowy curtain floating in a summer's breeze. But now, as close as we are standing to one another, I can see the tiny details that make Holly a complete knockout. I manage to see the light smattering of freckles as they spread out across the bridge of her nose. I trace the perfect cupid's bow of her upper lip with my eyes, take in her dark, black hair that is currently not straight but not curly in the way my sister's is. My eyes continue to take in the tattoos that seem to cover more skin than what has been left untouched—too numerous to count in any one sitting. They drink in her little upturned nose that is similar to my sister's in size and shape. I admire her narrow hips and full cleavage, her collarbone begging to be left with marks—a not-so-gentle reminder of the one night when we came together to give Noel the one thing she has always wanted.

I nod toward the scarf at the end of the table before dropping into a chair nestled into the corner of the kitchen. At first, it seemed out of place, but as I watched the snow outside fall from the floor-to-ceiling window behind it earlier, I knew that it was placed with purpose. "Let's start with that." Patting my lap, I turn all my attention to my sister. "Come here, Baby Girl. Sit on my lap and let's discover together what type of toys you want Santa to bring you this year."

Again and again, I remind myself that this is likely her first experience with true kink. That at the age of eighteen, it's likely she has never had more than a silky blindfold wrapped around her eyes in the heat of passion, that what I am giving her tonight—if she continues to trust me after seeing what I want to do to her—is something often seen as extreme to people who don't participate in the lifestyle.

Noel drops into my lap slowly, as if she is afraid of me.

Perhaps she is.

Before she can fully seat herself on top of me, I place a hand on each hip and bring her against me in one swift movement. "I don't know what either of you enjoy most when it is just the two of you, so in the interest of not wanting to push you outside of your comfort zone, we're starting with the basics. Over the course of the night, I'm going to ask you for a color, and you're going to tell me green if things are good, yellow if you need me to slow down or back off, and red if you need me to stop immediately. If something makes you uncomfortable—either of you," I look away from my sister to meet Holly's eyes, "say red, and everything stops without question. And while I'm going to ask you, to check in with you—you never need to wait for me to ask you to call red. Hell, even yellow, for that matter."

Both women nod, but it isn't enough. "Words, ladies. You're both going to have to use your words today. Holly, what color are you?"

"Green," she replies quickly, catching my eye and communicating that she understands how important it is to lay out this groundwork before diving into the main event.

"And you, my sweet sister. What's your color, Baby Girl?" I

nuzzle into the crook of her neck, inhaling the sweet, pepper-mint smell that radiates from her year-round.

"Green," she says. "Really fucking green."

I chuckle at the enthusiastic consent, knowing it might not stay that way much longer. "Now tell me, if Holly were to tease your body with that scarf—sliding the fabric over your smooth skin," I nod toward my sister, and Holly takes my cue, coming to stand in front of where we are both seated. Gently, she runs the scarf over my sister's arms, bare except for the thinnest straps holding up her nightshirt. Holly trails the fabric over Noel's creamy thighs and back up to lightly caress the exposed skin of her neck "What color would that be?"

Without hesitation, Noel supplies her answer. "Green."

Again and again, we complete the same thing with the various implements I have scrounged up from around the house. I find myself proud of my sister when she deems all the things I've shown her as acceptable, despite the fact that I could still see the fear on her pretty face when I slapped her open palm with the back of the flat hairbrush, giving her only an idea of the sensation it could produce against her bare ass.

She has absolutely no idea how long I've had fantasies of turning her ass nice and red. And while most of them have come in the form of my bare hand against her bare ass—that feeling of skin against skin that has always been such a turn-on to me—I can't deny that the loud *thwack* of the brush against her palm was enough to make my dick jump on its own accord while my sadistic little heart gave out a pitter patter of an almost musical beat I've never felt before.

The entire time, Holly has been nearby, serving as my kinky assistant. Bringing me implements as I ask for them, gently speaking to my sister in a smooth cadence that seems to ground her, and reminding her to check in with her colors as we move from item to item.

We talk about hard limits and soft limits, and both Holly

and myself look at my sister in shock when she confesses that her dream is to have both of us fill her at once.

And when Holly leaves the room momentarily, off to retrieve a strap-on from her luggage, I use the moment to once again check in with my sister one-to-one.

Shifting her in my lap, I drape her feet over the side of the oversized chair while keeping her ass firmly in place. I desperately need to be able to see her face—to read what's going on in her mind by looking deep into those green eyes that are currently as dark as the pine needles from the Christmas tree just several feet away in the living room. "You still good, sweetheart?"

She gives me a smile that could melt the heart of the grinchiest grinch that ever grinched, and I can't help but pull her closer, dropping a kiss to her forehead in a rarely-shown form of affection. "I'm good," she says softly. "Better than I ever thought possible when I was guided into the kitchen backward and turned around to see your grumpy face sitting on a barstool."

Together, we laugh for what is probably the first time ever —me holding her to my body while one of her hands reaches up to tangle in my slightly unkempt hair. It's even more electric, the energy swirling around us as we wait for Holly's return, than it was just a few short hours ago when our lips touched for the first time.

"And you're sure that the two of you can handle this— bringing someone else into your bed for the night?"

"For once in your life, can you please trust that I know what is best for myself and for my relationships? She might be the first person I've ever been with, but I know what I want—what I *need* to experience. To know if these feelings I have inside of me have anything to do with the insatiable need I have to claim you and the insatiable need I have for you to claim me. I can have you for one night, and I've come to terms with that. Let me deal with my own consequences."

Simultaneously, I register Noel's words at the same exact time Holly reenters the room with a harness and multiple silicone dildos in her hands in an assortment of colors and shapes and...appendages.

Tentacles...who knew?

I shake my head, trying to bring myself back to what my stepsister just said.

She's only ever been with one person before.

She's never been with a man before.

She wants me to be the first.

And I don't know what causes me to do it, because I should be thrilled by this news. Thrilled by the fact that I'll be the first cock to slide between her legs, the first cock to press against her pouty mouth, and the first cock to push past that tight ring of muscle as I stretch her ass, readying her to take every single inch of me.

But I'm not jumping for joy at the news.

In fact, I'm fucking terrified.

My voice is shaky when I say it, but I know it needs to happen.

The one single word that can bring it all to a stop.

"Red."

SIX

"What the fuck do you mean, red?" Noel asks, pushing up from my lap to stand over me. She's laughing, likely assuming this is a joke on my part. After all, after over a decade, we were finally starting to thaw the ice that has always kept us away from one another. Ice that *I* had cautiously placed between us to save both of us from acting irrationally. And you know, to save me from the possibility of a lengthy prison sentence for fucking a minor.

But I digress.

Her eyes bounce between mine, the laughter falling from her face to quickly be replaced by a scowl when she sees the closed-off body language I've reverted back to. "You're not fucking serious, Saint? All because I've never fucked a man before?"

Holly watches us, the silicone cocks and tentacle still gripped in her hands bringing the only ounce of comedic levity to this situation.

"This is fucking incredulous!" she shouts, her voice becoming shrill. "We go through all of this bullshit," her hand waves toward the table, where the random household items still lay scattered across the surface, "and you can't even fucking go through with it."

Stalking to the table, she picks up a clothespin and throws it at me.

Batting it away before it smacks me square in the face, I push up to my full height, towering over Noel, who keeps her eyes locked on me with such an angry fury that I worry she is about to turn me to ash.

"Was this always some game to you, Saint? Just another way to play with my emotions? Another way to run away from what scares you?" She comes closer and closer to me, never breaking eye contact as she continues to hurl clothespin after clothespin at my head.

One bounces off my chest, another hitting my shoulder, and still, the assault continues.

"Why, Saint, *why*?" Her voice is strained, as if she's trying to keep the tears from falling. "Why is it so hard for you to love me the way I know only you're capable of? Why is it so hard for you to *love*?"

Noel, never one to back down from a fight—even when I'm clearly trying to retreat—advances on me with each step until we're chest to chest. Though over a head shorter than I am, her tenacity is fierce, and when she reaches out to slap me across the face—for the second time in less than twenty-four hours—I'm thankful for Holly's interference, knowing that this time, I would have certainly ended up with a Noel-sized handprint across my cheek.

"Come on, my sweet girl." Wrapping a hand around my sister's bicep, she pulls her away with little resistance. "Why don't we go upstairs and cool down for a little bit?"

With even less of a fight, Noel allows Holly to guide her out of the kitchen. It isn't until the pair reach the base of the stairs that lead to the second level that my sister turns back toward me, the tears evident in her big, mossy green eyes.

Turning with more force than a tornado cutting through a dilapidated farmhouse, I punch the padded armchair I was previously sitting in before collapsing back into the soft fabric it provides.

With my head in my hands, I replay Noel's words again and again, wondering if perhaps, I really am unable to love.

I'm not sure how long I sit there, the minutes ticking by in an anamorphosis display of just how twisted time can be.

Footfalls on the stairs have my attention turning toward the sound. I find Holly descending with no sight of my sister.

She's changed into a pair of flannel pajama bottoms with little Christmas trees of different colors and a simple, black, long-sleeve shirt that looks exceptionally soft. Her hair is up and off her face, piled high on top of her head in one of those fancy buns that look like they took ten seconds when you know in actuality it took time to achieve the perfect, messy look.

Without asking for permission, she plops onto my lap as if it is the most natural thing in the world. As if I wasn't just entering into a screaming match with the woman she loves. The smell of cinnamon wafts around us as she makes herself comfortable, reminding me of gingerbread cookies fresh from the oven.

"Wanna talk about it?" she asks, no trace of sarcasm in her tone.

However I look at the situation, I can tell there is no getting out of being forced to open up to this still near-stranger. No skirting around the issues that have continually pulled me and Noel apart while pushing us back together with near fatal consequences. "Do I even have a choice?" I bite back, slightly more hostile than intended.

She lets out a little sigh. "Consent isn't just about what happens in the bedroom. After the little display of showmanship for your sister's benefit, I would think you would know that better than most. I won't force you to talk to me, Saint. I know I don't seem like a neutral party here, but despite what you think, I really do have both of your best interests in hand."

"What are you? Some kind of therapist or some shit?" I ask, suddenly interested in what makes this woman think she can fix whatever issues there are between myself and my sister that have caused us to fight like fucking cats and dogs since the day we first met.

Holly laughs, the sound breaking some of the tension that has been swirling in the open kitchen since before Noel stormed out. "Yeah, I'm studying to become a therapist...or some shit. I actually focus on adult conflict resolution, so I know a thing or two about difficult relationships."

"So, that's what this is for you then? A case study in dysfunctional familial relationships and how the holidays increase the stress on already fraught situations?"

She studies me for a minute, her blue eyes scrutinizing me with an intensity that makes my skin prickle with aware-ness. "And you think that I offered to sleep with you just to dupe your sister into being happy so I could *study* your fucked up family dynamic? That I was going to use you for part of my dissertation or something? Christ, maybe you are delusional."

Holly tries to push up from the chair, but I keep her locked in place, determined to understand her position in all of this mess—to understand why she seems just as desperate for a night with both myself and my sister as Noel seems for a night with me and Holly. "Then explain it to me, Little Girl. Explain to me why a beautiful woman such as yourself would want to share? Why you would want to watch as a man runs his hands over the breasts that belong to your woman? Why you would want to stand nearby as a man pushes his cock deep into the mouth that belongs to your lover, using that spit and saliva to fuck deep into the throat that should be saved for you and you alone? What do you get from thinking of someone else sliding into that undoubtedly tight cunt that hasn't been stretched by a real, flesh and blood cock?"

Undeterred, Holly doesn't throw some bratty retort in my face. Instead, a quiet little mewl slips from her mouth as her ass grinds against my lap.

Interesting.

"What's that, sweetheart? Does the idea of watching me with Noel actually turn you on?"

Again, she rocks against my lap, my rapidly hardening dick joining back in on the fun.

How the hell I've been able to go from soft to hard so fucking fast, I'll never know.

"I'm a fucking voyeur, Saint. Of course it turns me on. It doesn't matter if it is a man or a woman touching Noel, doesn't matter if it is one night of mind-blowing fun or a long-term deal where we're all equals." Holly twists in my lap, tossing a leg over each side to straddle me face-to-face. "Thinking of holding your sweet, little stepsister—her back against my chest as you continue to rock into her again and again." She presses her chest flush against my own, leaning in to graze her teeth down the side of my neck in a near-painful ecstasy. "I'd be lying if I said I haven't thought about it time and time again since Noel first mentioned you'd be here for the holidays. I just never expected it would actually be an option."

I study her face for a moment, not giving anything away that's going on in my own mind. It makes her nervous, her weight slightly shifting in my lap.

Or maybe she's just trying to find more friction? Trying to find a way to grind what is surely a pretty, greedy little pussy against the growing length in my pants.

But it doesn't matter what I say to my sister. At this point, I don't think there is anything I can do to bring her back from the crushing blow I dealt to her less than an hour ago.

As if she can read my thoughts, Holly speaks once again, a

hand coming up to run through my hair while she looks me in the eye with a cautious optimism I don't quite feel myself. "I took a bath with her while we were upstairs. I got her changed into something comfortable and told her I was coming back downstairs to make dinner for us—that she should rest and I'd come to get her when it was time to eat. Go to her, Saint. Show her that you can be everything she wants you to be—even if just for one night."

I stare back in shock at what I think she is insinuating. "You want me to go upstairs and fuck my sister. Without you?"

"Do you remember what it was like growing up with the last name Klaus?" When I don't immediately answer, she continues—as if she was hoping I wouldn't. "Trust me, I get it more than most. Do you know what it was like to grow up with the last name Yule?"

The name smacks me right in the middle of the forehead like an icy snowball that you know will leave a mark. "You're Holly Yule?"

With a flourish of her wrist, she gives me a mock bow from her perch atop my lap. "The one and only."

If the Klaus family name is synonymous with Christmas toys, the Yule family is the exact same—only their name conjures images of priceless antique glass baubles and bows that usually become family heirlooms being passed down from generation to generation. Their year-round Christmas window display on Fifth Avenue makes national headlines for its over-the-top grandeur at least once a year, usually in the weeks leading up to the busy Christmas shopping season.

Holly doesn't let her family's surname sink in for long before she continues once again. "I grew up on my own. Sure, my mom and dad are still together—still going strong when countless people have betted against them over the years. But that's the thing, Saint. My mom and dad—they have each other and the business that was passed on to my father just like it was passed on to his father before him. They never wanted a little bough of Holly. Never cared if I was naughty or nice. That loneliness I felt growing up? You felt it too, Saint, didn't you?" I nod, my head moving on its own accord at her voodoo magic words that hit me in the chest, the last of my walls tumbling down into a dusty pile of rubble. "And if both of us did, there is a very real possibility that Noel felt it, too. That she *still* feels it."

God, to be able to feel like I'm something for one night—to feel like I'm *somebody*. Not just Saint Klaus, heir to the unwanted Klaus toy fortune. Not just a tortuous older brother to the bratty little sister who has forced me to run away in fear time and time again.

Leaning forward, I capture Holly's lips with mine for the first time. It's a thank you and a promise all rolled into one. It's the knowledge that tonight, the trio of us will feel anything but alone. That despite our last names and the situations that are stacked against us—that prevent us from being our true selves as we were engineered to be by some higher power—that tonight, we can have it all without anything standing in our way.

We break apart, spending a moment with our foreheads pressed tightly to one another. We speak without words, without apprehension or disdain for one another.

And finally...fucking *finally*...I see that showing up here a few days early and running into these two beautiful women who have many more layers I've yet to uncover is exactly where I want to be this Christmas.

SEVEN

The room is dim when I enter, the glow from a nearby salt lamp the only light to lead my way. Quietly, I close the door behind me, only sparing a moment to look around the over-sized room before I pad across the floor in an equally as silent movement.

I'm not sure how I ended up in what appears to be a room for an eighty-year-old geriatric, but the room Noel and Holly have chosen for themselves is as different as night and day.

Large windows line one wall, their black-out curtains drawn to protect against the sun that has yet to begin its nightly descent, making way for the moon to come out and play. The four-poster bed, at least a king–if not larger–sits proudly against the far wall of the room, soft gray linens piled high to protect against the bitter, often frozen landscape just outside the front door to the chalet masquerading as a cabin.

In the middle of the bed, I can barely make out the form of a body under the layers of blankets—the form lightly rising and falling with each breath my sister takes. I watch her easy movements, the steady inhale and exhale, taking some solace in the fact that she is resting, while silently resenting myself for bringing her so much hurt over the years since we were thrown together with no help from the adults in our lives.

We were never set up for success as a family—as brother and sister—and it has done nothing but hurt us in the long run.

The mattress dips below my weight as I sit next to her, nearly chuckling at her adorable appearance when my eyes land on her face. Her hair is styled similarly to Holly's, pieces of corkscrew curls hanging around her face as if they escaped the locked prison of the hair elastic. Her mouth is slightly parted, a light snore escaping with every third breath she takes. Impossibly long eyelashes fan out over her cheeks, and in this moment, she looks at peace.

Trying my hardest not to wake her just yet, I gently move the blankets from around her, drawing in a shuddered breath when I see what awaits.

Noel Belle—bane of my existence, temptress of all teases, sassy sexpot on legs—is wearing one of *my* shirts.

It's an old shirt, one of the few shirts left over from my days at college. It must have been forgotten two years prior when I fled our Hampton home in haste, desperate to get away from the temptation I so misguidedly saw as hatred.

But now, as she lays in front of me in a thin, navy shirt with my alma mater scrawled across the front in large, block letters, I know that Holly was right.

Noel was never testing me because she wanted me to get in trouble. She was never trying to tease me or torment me. She simply wanted someone to give her the attention she so desperately needed as a young girl. Even now at eighteen, it's almost smack-me-in-the-face obvious. I only hate that it took another person to point it out to me, to open my eyes to the fact that perhaps, while my darling little stepsister does have the tendencies of almost every brat I've ever tamed, she was simply in need of the most basic of human needs—attention and affection.

Even more shocking is how much I crave *her* attention and affection now that I understand the motives behind her actions.

With my mind made up, I slide under the blankets next to her before pulling her close to my body. Noel is beyond warm —her skin toasty to the touch from the multiple blankets piled high on the bed—and the thought of sliding into her cunt while she's just as warm between the legs yet still fast asleep flashes through my mind.

But that isn't something I can do tonight.

Or ever.

Because despite the fact that I'm ready for this—ready to share this private moment with my stepsister before we return to the ground level and share in a night of passion with Holly— that's still all it can ever be.

One night.

A single night in the grand scheme of our lives doesn't sound like much, but I already know that this night—*fuck*, it means everything to Noel. And for some reason, I'm beginning to think it means something to Holly and myself, too.

With slow and steady strokes, I begin to slide my hands up and down Noel's body. I smooth over the fabric of my shirt that looks better on her than it ever looked on me before I slide my hand all the way down to the hem of the shirt where it sits bunched up around her thighs. The skin of my hand feels rough against her own supple body, and it makes me greedy for more.

I bite back a groan when she stirs, pressing her tight, little ass against my dick. Likely expecting her lover, she gasps when she feels my stiff shaft and hard body.

"Sa...Saint?" she asks, voice still thick with sleep.

My fingers trail up further, skirting past her thighs and bypassing the one place I want so desperately to bury my face into while seeking salvation. I pull her body closer to mine, rocking against her ass with eager thrusts. "*Shhhh*, I'm here

Baby Girl. I promise, no running this time. I'll never run again."

Noel turns over, facing me with wide yet slightly hesitant eyes. There is so much fear in those eyes. So much distrust and hurt.

I chastise myself, knowing the only person I have to blame is myself.

If I pull her any closer to me, she'll physically be able to crawl into my soul.

Part of me thinks she's already there.

Slowly, so fucking slow that a Goddammed snail could outpace me, I pull the oversized shirt up her body, taking a full minute to admire the gorgeous sight in front of me. My large hands come out to grasp at her hips, pulling her on top of me until she is sitting upright, one leg perched on either side of my torso.

Noel doesn't hesitate when I lift the shirt over her head, depositing it somewhere on the mattress to be found at a different time and place. She doesn't try to hide her body or shield her beauty from my greedy eyes, and I drink in her form, backlit in the gentle glow of the room like a well-deserved star at the top of the brightest tree in the neighborhood.

"Please," she gasps as my hands come up to cup her breasts, the pads of my thumbs sweeping across the already tight peaks of her rosy, pink nipples. "Don't run away from me again. I was so lonely, Saint. *Please*, don't leave me alone again."

"I'm here now, Baby Girl." My hands never stop exploring her skin, never stop tracing patterns over her arms and thighs, over her stomach and ass. "Let me make it all better—let me make you feel all better."

"Holly…" she starts, but I pull her down to my lips, her tits pressing against my chest, and cut her off with a kiss.

"Holly is the one who convinced me to come up here—to

make things right with you. My name might be Saint, but she's the true angel."

The smile she flashes at me in return is downright devious. "Do you remember what I said to you two years ago?"

"No." I feign innocence, but from the laughter bubbling out my sister's mouth, I know that she knows I'm full of shit. Especially considering it isn't the first time *The Incident* has been spoken about today.

Her hips roll against my length. Once, twice, three, times she rocks against me, coaxing me through the fabric of my sleep pants, the heat of her cunt searing into my body. "Can you make me feel good now...Daddy?"

A low growl comes from somewhere deep inside my chest. I have Noel lifted off my lap long enough to shed my pants before removing my shirt, adding them both to the growing pile of clothing now littering the oversized room. "Say it again, Baby Girl."

I tease her with the head of my cock—angry and red and leaking with anticipation. Up and down, I slide it through her pussy, coating it in her own, natural lubrication before using the head of my cock to draw small, lazy circles on her clit.

"Please, Daddy," she pants, already close to falling over the edge. "Just do it, Saint. Let me feel you stretch me."

Her words fuel something deep within me, the need to claim her overwhelming all my senses. Still straddling my lap, Noel lines herself up with my cock. "You on the pill, sweetheart?"

She nods, barely finishing before she's impaling herself on my length. While she's ridden those fake dicks I last saw downstairs, this is her first time with the real thing and I know I should take it slow, to let her get used to my size. The comparison between the real thing, and what Holly can provide her is something I'll never know for myself, yet I know I have to make this good for her. Make this *perfect* for her. My fingers reach out to find purchase on her hips, every ounce of my self-control going into keeping myself still, from not ramming into her so hard that my cock comes out of her Goddammed mouth. "Take it slow, Baby Girl. There's no rush."

"That's where you're wrong." Placing a palm on each of my pecs, she steadies herself against my chest as she tries desperately to move her hips—to sink onto more of my cock. "We're on borrowed time, Saint, and I'm not letting a minute go to waste. So let me ride your dick until you come deep inside me. Because I can't think of anything hotter than going downstairs to have dinner with the woman I love with your seed dripping down the inside of my thighs."

Fuck. Me.

I reach up, harshly pinching each nipple between my thumb and forefinger until she's gasping for air. Until she's wiggling and squirming, now fully seated on my length. "What's your color, Baby Girl?"

Hips slowly rocking up into her, she groans out her response. "Green, Daddy."

And that's all it takes.

Pulling her body to my chest, I roll us until Noel ends up on the bottom, my cock still deep inside of her. With a hand on each calf, I spread her wide, pull out almost all the way, and slam back into her cunt.

The clenching is near instant, her walls wanting to keep me buried deep within her pussy just as badly as my dick wants to live out the rest of its life in the same place.

I pound into her with a strength and force that could start an avalanche outside our door. Fuck it, let the snow bury us— give us a reason to stay here forever.

I pour my anger into her—the frustration for the years we lost, the hurt that flickers across her face when she thinks that no one is looking. I pour my desire into her—the deep-seated need that takes root within my soul with each and every thrust to keep her forever. To say fuck it to everyone with any expectations. To find some way to make whatever is happening between the two of us—no, the *three* of us—work.

My sister sobs beneath me, a chorus of *thank you* and *I always knew you'd come for me* mixed in with a smattering of *please* and a dash of *more*. It's as if she's calling out the ingredients to the perfect sugar cookie, only this recipe is the key to her desire, and it's a recipe I'm determined to memorize, never wanting to forget the feeling of the first time Noel Belle came apart under my body.

She's boneless in my arms, her calves weighing heavy in my hands, yet I continue to pound into her, my own words of affirmation coming in a litany of *good girl* and *you take my cock so well* with blessings of *I'm so fucking sorry* and *this is only the beginning* trailing closely behind as I spill into her on a roar, only one thought playing on repeat in my mind.

After tonight, my life will never be the same.

EIGHT

Dinner was beyond wonderful. A delicious meal of seared salmon and asparagus so fresh, I would have sworn it was straight from the farm as opposed to the late-season delicacy it actually is. Thankfully, unlike me, my sister had the foresight to stock up the cabin before she arrived, and lucky for the both of us, I discovered after taking my first bite of food that Holly had a few semesters of failed culinary school under her belt—having had given it a shot prior to finding her true calling in the field of psychology.

Perhaps what surprises me even more is that my sister—resident party girl always at the ready to pose for tabloid fodder and gossip magazines—is going to school with dreams of being a pediatrician.

Who would have thought?

Certainly not me. But then again, maybe that's because I've truly never taken the time to get to know her before now.

Throughout dinner, I can't take my eyes off both of the women who sit across from one another, having allowed me to take my place at the head of the table where I can cast my gaze over their bodies in a greedy yet appreciative way. From the first bite of the salad course—dark, slightly bitter greens with a honey-mustard vinaigrette—to our last bite of decadent dessert —a chocolate cake in individual mugs that ooze melted caramel when you break through the top—we get to know each other.

I laugh along with the pair as they recount the story of how they met—my sister walking into the wrong class on her first day as a freshman in college, being too afraid to disrupt the class by getting up and walking away, and settling into a chair next to Holly, who was a junior at the time. It serendipitously was the only open seat in a lecture hall of almost five hundred students, and by the end of the class, my sister was smitten and had sent an email to her advisor to permanently change her schedule to include the class she had wandered into on accident without a clue of what it meant for the rest of her life.

It's...cute?

We talk about heavier topics, commiserating over the shared loneliness we felt as the children of the rich and famous. Not ever truly neglected yet still lacking in more ways than one. We talk of the private schools we attended and the galas where we rubbed elbows with powerful men and women from around the world before any of us were old enough to truly understand the magnitude of the lives we were born into without our consent.

First-world problems, sure. But problems nonetheless.

And when I find out that my sister, the object of so much misplaced aggression that has rapidly shifted to need and desire and want, spent last Christmas and her eighteenth birthday without our parents at her side, I physically have to remove myself from the house.

Stumbling upon a shed off the brick patio that's been buried under substantial snowfall, I cast a glance toward the jacuzzi where I first saw Noel before I continue to the shed, pulling an axe from the depths of its bones and chopping wood for nearly an hour non-stop. I swing that axe as piece after piece of wood shatters around me, not stopping to stack it into a neat and tidy pile to be used as heating for the large home. I swing that axe as I curse my father—curse him for neglecting the most beautiful gift he was ever given. I swing that axe as I hurl matching curses toward Noel's mother, abandoning her daughter alone while continually chasing her own vapid happiness and success. I swing that axe, and I swing that axe, and I swing that axe until I think I'm about to collapse, my vision going dark around the edges.

"Saint!"

Her voice cuts through the air, the only other sound aside from the *thwack, thwack, thwack* of my axe as it meets wood again and again and again.

It's Holly, coming to find me in next to nothing but the look of concern on her face. "Come inside with me. Now."

For someone like myself who is used to giving the commands, it feels strange to obey her without question. Yet, for some reason, my body tells me not to argue, that in this moment, I don't have to be in charge. And I take the respite while I can.

I toss the axe onto the snowy ground, not bothering to return it to the shed, before I link my fingers through Holly's outstretched hand, allowing her to lead me back into the house.

We bypass the main living space, the sound of my sister washing dishes as she softly sings Christmas Carols filling the house. We use a secondary staircase that I hadn't seen until now, leaving me to wonder what other secret passageways exist within the walls of this place. Trailing behind Holly, she guides me into the room I was in just a few hours ago, on top of and under Noel. I expect her to stop at the bed, but she continues until we enter the oversized bathroom, more apt for a resort spa than a house.

Holly turns the tap on the enormous tub, dropping a few round-looking balls into the water that begin to fizz the moment they make contact. The smell of cinnamon, clove, and honey fill the air as steam rises from the water, and I find my muscles begin to relax with each deep inhalation I take. Turning back to me, Holly silently helps me undress—pulling the Henley and sleep pants from my body—before instructing me to get into the tub by gesturing to it with her hand.

When she believes the water has hit an acceptable level, she turns the tap off before gesturing for me to scoot forward–still silent, still only using her body language to guide me.

If anything, I would have expected her to slide between my legs, not to take the position behind me. Yet when I lay back against her breasts, her arms coming up to wrap around me, lazily leaving rivulets of water in their wake, I melt into her embrace.

"It sucks," she says quietly against the shell of my ear, finally breaking the heavy silence that had grown between us. "To grow up the way we did—to feel like we had absolutely everything but nothing all at once. It takes a lot to let go of the resentment, to move forward. You'll get there, too. If you choose to do so."

I should hate that she has me figured out so easily. How she can see just how utterly broken I am underneath the tough exterior.

Yet it doesn't.

Instead, I feel seen.

For once in my fucking life, I feel seen and validated.

And God*damn*, do I want to feel this way more often.

"Teach me," I tell her on a shaky exhale, well aware that my eyes are misting over, a reaction I've never had once in my twenty-four years. "Teach me how to let it go. To not be so angry all the time, to love."

In the most vulnerable moment of my life—more so than me slipping into bed next to my sleeping stepsister—I sit motionless as Holly wraps a hand around my shaft. I'm already half-hard, despite the less-than-sexual nature of our discussion, and as she gives me slow, lazy strokes, I harden further until I'm fully erect. Sliding back and forth, her palm caresses me, and that combined with the warm water of the tub creates a satisfying sensation I could easily get lost in.

"I wish I could fuck it out of you," she croons in my ear, her hot breath sending shivers across my skin. "And while that would be exceptionally enjoyable for both of us, what you need is to talk to someone who *isn't* me."

"Why can't it be you?" My voice comes out strained as she continues to pump my cock, her grip tightening slightly with each downward stroke.

Holly's other hand disappears into the water, gently tugging on my balls. "For starters, I'm not licensed yet." She pauses for a moment, as if in deep thought. "And you know, I think I remember my professor in Psychology 101 explicitly stating that it *is* frowned upon for me to fuck my patients—and I plan on doing *a lot* of that tonight, Saint."

The menace grazes her nails up my shaft, and every muscle in my body contracts, trying to hold off the urge I have to blow like a mother-fucking volcano that's been lying dormant for centuries. "Christ, woman, are you trying to talk me into therapy by controlling my orgasms? You keep doing that and this is going to be over way too soon."

"*Mhmmm*, that wasn't what I was getting at, but I can't say that I hate the thought." I can't see her face in this position, but I can tell she is smiling just from her voice, and it makes me grin in response. "Orgasm denial? Oh, or maybe forced orgasms over and over again until you can't come anymore? Till it physically hurts to get hard? Till you agree to take care of yourself so you can learn to take care of your sister?"

"This is just for tonight, and you know it. It's you who will give her the aftercare she needs—to continue to take care of her long after this holiday is over."

"Sweet, sweet Saint." Holly's voice is huskier now, a smoke-like rasp coating each and every syllable as she speaks. "You don't have to lie to me, Saint. Did you really expect this to only ever be *one* night?"

"Yes," I tell her.

But she hears the hesitation, just as I do.

Thankfully, Holly lets the topic go, nuzzling into my neck, her hand starting to stroke me faster—with more urgency. "One night or forever, there *is* something I desperately want to see right now. What I want for Christmas this year is to watch you erupt all over my hand right here in this tub—your cum mixing with the water, the after-effects of our twisted game floating along the surface as a dirty little reminder of what we've done.

"And when you're spent and recovered, maybe I want you to take me into the bedroom and tie me to the chair that's sitting in the corner. Maybe I want you to bring Noel upstairs to our room. And only when we're all in the same room again, do I want you to use her body however you want, bringing her to climax again and again until she is begging you for mercy. Until her pussy is extra pink and puffy from use, till your cum is leaking down her thighs for days."

Fucking hell.

She paints a pretty picture, and my hips begin to thrust against her movement as I play the scene out in my head, wanting more of whatever it is she is willing to give me. "You're a kinky fucking bitch, aren't you?"

Her laugh is devious as her grip tightens around me once more, the first spurt of my release mixing into the water. "You have no fucking idea, Saint. But I think what's even more exciting is that even if it is just for one night like you so desperately want to trick yourself into believing, that for tonight—I'm *your* kinky fucking bitch."

I'm not sure how it happened, but somehow, I definitely ended up on the nice list this year.

NINE

Positioning the chair that I've pulled to the middle of the room facing the bed, I gesture to Holly, inviting her to get comfortable.

It's a simple, wooden chair, almost more suited for a dining room than a bedroom, but it allows me to work quickly and safely. And while we talked through all of Holly and Noel's limits earlier in the day, I'm careful to explain what I'm doing to Holly as I work to tie her in place in a way that doesn't detract from the act of intimacy that is happening between the two of us right now.

Rope play is a powerful tool when used effectively. It can make your partner feel many things—sweet and sexy to devilish and debauched. And it can be extremely seductive both with *and* without the actual act of sex. Just as it can be as seductive to be the partner doing the rigging—tying rope around a person—as it is to be the one having the rope tied around them.

Yet tonight, something feels different. Sure, I'm used to being the rigger in a rope play scene. And while I'm worshiping every inch of Holly's body like I would any other play partner in her position, tonight it doesn't feel like I am giving her the honor to be in her position as much as I feel like she has bestowed the honor on me. Like being on my knees in front of this woman to loop Christmas garland around her perfect tits and cute waist is a gift she has given me.

And God*damn* do I feel like a lucky son-of-a-bitch for it.

With a simple chest harness to start, I loop the excess garland around the slats on the back of the chair, already beginning to restrict how far Holly can move. "When did you know she was the one? That you loved her?"

She beams at me, and I take in the calmness of the moment. The way we're able to talk as we work through this together— setting up the perfect scene for not only my sister but for Holly as well.

All too frequently, people confuse sex and kink, believing that the two have to be mutually exclusive with one another. They think that it is about seriousness and power, that it is all whips and chains and floggers, that it's all forbidden and harsh.

And sure, all those things can make up an amazing scene, but there can also be lightness and levity and laughter.

And this is the perfect example, as I trail red, sparkly garland over her body, building up the anticipation and tickling her senses while reminding her that soon, the woman she loves will be in front of her, getting fucked as she's forced to sit tied to this chair without being able to do a single fucking thing about it.

It's kinky as fuck, and my dick isn't even anywhere near her pussy.

Yet.

Because sure, sex and kink don't have to be mutually beneficial, but when kink and sex are combined, it can be downright explosive. And tonight, I'm playing with a dangerously short fuse.

"She baked me a cake for my birthday." Holly laughs, and I momentarily pause my constant wrapping and teasing of the garland to lock eyes with her. "Neither of my parents remembered. And it shouldn't have surprised me, but for some reason, it did. I broke down in between classes when I realized another year would pass without as much as a phone call from them, and your sister found me in the hall with mascara tracks running down my cheeks. She pulled me into a nearby bathroom, ran a paper towel under the faucet before wiping my face clean, then made sure I got to my next class on time because I had a huge test the same day that I simply could not fail. Later that night, I was laying on the couch in my apartment, still feeling sorry for myself, and she showed up on my doorstep complete with a chocolate cake and those trick candles. You know the kind, the more you blow on them, the more they relight?

"And I'll tell you what, Saint. That cake was fucking *awful*. I think she used baking powder when she was supposed to use baking soda, and I know for a fact that she used almond extract instead of vanilla. The frosting was lumpy, and the entire thing tasted faintly metallic, but it was the single best cake of my life because she made it for me."

"She saw you when no-one else did," I say absentmindedly.

Holly nods, repeating my own words back to me. "She saw *you* when no-one else did."

I only wish it didn't take me so long to realize it.

Leaning in, I press a kiss to her lips before trailing the garland across her body, tying a simple rope shackle around each wrist. "You're pretty incredible. Thank you for being there for her—you know, when I was too stupid to see it for myself."

She rolls her eyes and I use the moment to break through the seriousness of the moment. "Your brat is showing, little girl. Might want to tuck that back in."

Her laugh is magical, filling the space between us.

I can see the allure of Holly Yule.

Those big, blue eyes that are deceptively innocent. The way

she can reach deep into your soul to pull out your deep-seated insecurities with a simple look.

Not being able to hold back, I lean forward and kiss her again, this time with more force. Tasting the barest hint of chocolate still on her tongue from our dessert, I pull back and look into her eyes, willing her to see just how much of my truth she has already seen tonight. Far more than I've ever shown anyone before.

"You're going to be a great therapist," I tell her.

And I mean it truthfully.

Retrieving another length of garland, I turn my own eyes on Holly, scanning her body as an idea forms. "How adventurous are you feeling tonight?"

"What did you have in mind?" she responds with an equally as flirtatious cadence to her voice.

Repeating a process I've done hundreds of times, I fold the garland in half—just as I would with any other rope specifically tailored to bondage. Finding the very center of the length of red, festive material, I trail the end over her pussy, still covered by a scrap of fabric no larger than a postage stamp on a Christmas wish list sent to Santa.

"I could affix your ankles to the legs of the chair, essentially rendering you immobile. You could leave your panties on and watch in agony as I play with my stepsister's perfect cunt right in front of you." With a hand on each ankle, I place her legs where they would be in this position, allowing her to try it out.

"What's my other option?" she asks, her voice breathy.

Releasing my hold on her ankles, I grab her hips and shift her to the edge of the chair, her ass nearly hanging over the side of the hard surface. I spread her legs—a hand on each calf —then slowly push her backward, essentially folding her in half. "Or I take off your panties that are certainly already drenched, tie your knees as well as your ankles to the back of the chair, and put your pussy on display so both Noel and I can see just how wet it makes you to watch her get fucked by me."

I barely finish my sentence when she is responding, "That option, that's the one I want."

Placing her feet back on the ground, I help to rid Holly of her panties, the full aroma of her desire hitting my nose when I bring the fabric to my nostrils and inhale. It makes me fucking salivate.

"You smell good, baby," I say, bringing her first leg up to lean against my shoulder, giving me easier access to place the multiple knots around her knees and ankles while supporting her weight. "I bet once I get you all tied up, that your pussy will already be wet for me, won't it?"

"You have such a filthy mouth. That's usually my job—the dirty talk."

I can't help myself, leaning down to bite her lightly on the inside of her thigh before I shift to the second leg, repeating the process. "Then be filthy with me, Holly. Use that filthy fucking mouth of yours to tell me exactly what you want to happen next. Because the more I get to know you, the more I'm starting to think you get off on being in charge just as much as you get off on watching."

Standing, I take in my work, reveling in the way Holly's body is on display for my eyes. Choosing to go sans top, she's completely naked, completely spread for me, and completely at my mercy with miles of tattooed flesh ready for the taking.

Of course, I was right, her pussy already shining with a light sheen of moisture from her desire. Dusky, pink nipples slightly darker than my sister's stand out against her skin in tight little peaks, her breasts framed in the red garland that suddenly seems to shimmer in the light.

I want to angle myself at the entrance of her pussy and slam into her without warning, making her scream into the quiet room around us.

I want to devour her cunt with my lips and tongue and teeth as she cries out her release, coating my tongue as I greedily drink in her arousal.

I want to leave bite marks on her breasts. Want to flog her, and cane her, and spank her until her ass resembles an oil spill —colors of reds and pinks and blues and purples spreading out under my palm as I massage her tender skin after being thoroughly worked over.

I want, I want, I *want*.

Rein it in, Saint. This isn't about you; it's about them.

Being the greedy fucker that I am, I can't control myself completely. Reaching down, I slide the pad of my thumb over her clit, loving the groan that leaves the back of her throat as I simply apply pressure to the most sensitive place on her body.

It should feel wrong—to be touching Holly like this after being with Noel just a few short hours ago. But if anything, it just makes me more excited to retrieve my sister from where she has been downstairs, blissfully unaware of what's unfolding above her.

Sliding my finger up and down Holly's pussy one single time, I coat my fingers in her juices and bring them up to taste, cursing at the sweet flavor of perfection on my tongue. "You feeling good? Nothing too tight? And you don't feel like anything is going to slip off anywhere?"

"All green, Saint. Go get our girl."

I throw a devious smile of my own over my shoulder, not entirely hating the way the phrase *our girl* sounds coming from Holly, and wondering if it would have the same allure to her if I was the one saying the words.

TEN

The gentle sound of Noel singing gives me pause as I reach the bottom of the main staircase.

Across the space, she's staring at the Christmas tree—a sad, longing look on her beautiful face as she sings Judy Garland's classic *Have Yourself A Merry Little Christmas* to no one in particular. As I watch from the last step, I'm taken back to the Christmas after we first became a family—her begging her mother with tears in her eyes to take her caroling like she had seen in many old Christmas movies while my father sat nearby, barking orders into his cellphone though it was nearly eight in the evening.

A cacophony of memories assault my senses. All the fancy dinners we were left out of, the times Noel cried as our parents left us once again, unable to be bothered by their duty as parents. I'm reminded of the times I felt equally as alone and now, as I watch the beautiful angel in front of me as she reaches out to touch an ornament, I feel like I have someone I can count on other than myself for the first time in my life.

Like, I could ask her for the world and she would give it to me. And not because she's a Belle and has more money than any one person could ever spend in a lifetime but because she truly would feel I was worthy of anything she had to offer.

I've been such a fucking asshole to her for years on end. Yet, she still finds herself drawn to me. Still finds herself craving me in the way I've always secretly craved her.

And I shouldn't even be considering it, but now, as I stand here watching her sing, unaware that she has an audience, I can't help but think of any possible scenario where I would be able to keep her—and not just Noel, but Holly, too—for more than tonight.

My feet take me to her without input from my brain, and I find myself wrapping my arms tightly around Noel from behind, pulling her closely to my chest. For the briefest of moments, she stiffens before she melts into me, allowing me to hold her tight.

We stare at the lights for a moment, neither of us speaking, yet so much is happening in the space between us.

Finally, I break the silence, knowing I left Holly just up the stairs and deliciously on display. "Come on, beautiful girl. I have something extra special for you upstairs."

Noel allows me to lead her up the steps, her hand in mine the entire way. It feels small enveloped in mine, her fingers so slim and smooth. So...*perfect*.

Chiding myself for even thinking it, I give her hand a squeeze as we come to stand in front of the door that is slightly ajar—just feet away from us. It blocks Noel's view of what's waiting for her on the other side, but from the way she now bounces on the balls of her feet, I can tell she's excited for what's to come—ever the young girl excited to tear open a present before Christmas day.

Hell, I can feel it vibrating from every cell of her body.

The excitement of the unknown seeps into my bones too, transferring through Noel and into my frame through the place where our hands remained linked. My face spreads into a wide smile, feeling as foreign against my skin as the excitement feels building in my body.

When I push open the door the rest of the way, I wait, allowing Noel to see the way Holly is on display for us for the first time.

The gasp that comes from my stepsister is worth every agonizing second it took to get us to this sick and twisted place where we stand now. We're both still at least partially clothed, but there's a bare cunt mere feet from where we stand, ready to be tortured and devoured and eaten like a Goddamned Christmas feast.

I knew it was obscene as I tied the garland around Holly's body again and again. Knew it was lascivious to have her spread wide, on display like a personal buffet. I knew it was primal to want to hold her down so she couldn't move her pretty, little body until I wanted her to.

And it seems like my darling little sister likes it every bit as much as I do.

Noel's breath has already picked up, coming in slow, deep waves that she works to keep measured. Her mossy green eyes flare when she turns to me, now nearly overcome by the darkness of pupils that have dilated to nearly fully eclipse the irises. "Can I...am I not allowed to touch her?"

It pleases me that she asks for permission so easily—as if it is a treat to follow her Daddy's rules.

In response, I nod toward Holly. "You can do whatever you'd like to her, Baby Girl—as long as it's within her limits. But before you do, wouldn't it be fun to tease her?" I continue talking to my sister as if Holly isn't in the room. Lightly, I rake my fingers down Noel's back, loving the way she shivers at my touch even with the thin fabric still separating us. "To climb on that bed and force her to watch as I feast on your juicy cunt? To watch her squirm as I palm your pretty, little tits and gorgeous, virgin ass? To see her dripping with arousal as I slide into your cunt that's only ever had one real cock inside of it—the cock that belongs to your filthy stepbrother?"

I shouldn't be as obsessed as I find myself when I picture my dick disappearing inside her pussy, I'm counting down the seconds until I can sink inside of her again with my real flesh that pulses and at times, moves of its own accord. Flesh that can erupt and mark and claim her from the inside out.

Holly moans from across the room while Noel quietly mewls next to me, trying to cover up the needy sound with a tiny cough. "Yes," my sister finally says, so quietly that I almost miss it. "I think I would like that a lot."

Without waiting a second longer, I sweep her into my arms, her legs immediately wrapping around my waist. I walk to the bed just like that—Noel wrapped tightly around my torso, my hands sliding up her back and into her hair as I take her mouth in a searing kiss. "I'm so fucked when it comes to you, Noel."

I'm not expecting a smile in response, but that's exactly what I get, and it is fucking magnificent. Fuck the star that led the wise men to the manger, Noel's smile is the only light I need.

Setting her on the bed, I position her body across the mattress, being sure Holly has a clear view. I look to the other woman, here but not allowed to participate of her own volition. "You doing okay over there, Little Girl?"

The smile she gives us in return is equally as bright as my sister's—a megawatt bulb in an otherwise dark night that's tinged with a bit of mischief. "Peachy. Now, are you going to show me what it's like when you mount my woman from behind and fuck her into oblivion, or are you going to keep checking in on us every five seconds?"

"You're lucky that you're over there and I'm otherwise occupied at the moment." I tug Noel's sleep shirt—*my shirt*—up and over her head, discarding it on the floor without a second glance. Sucking one of her nipples into my mouth, I swirl around the flesh, feeling it stiffen against my tongue. "Other-wise," I say, replacing my mouth with my fingers, lightly rolling her nipples between my thumb and forefinger of each hand, "I'd have to come over there and slap that pretty little face of yours for being such a brat. Now shut up and watch me fuck *our* beautiful baby girl into the mattress. Maybe if you're lucky, I'll let Noel lick your cunt clean when we're done."

If I'm expecting to feel something strange or off-kilter when I call Noel *our beautiful baby girl*, it never happens. In fact, it feels fucking amazing, my chest going tight at the words as emotion clogs my voice. To share her with Holly—equally as incredible in her own light.

Having her laid out across the mattress—both my gaze and Holly's roaming over her body before we lock eyes with one another—it feels like it could be the start of something magical, something *real*. Something more than one stupid night of passion between three adults who were expecting a quiet start to their holiday plans.

Not wasting any more time, I gesture for my sister to lay back, instructing her to keep her legs spread wide for me. "Remember, you're in control. You make the rules. If you need to stop for any reason at all, use your safe word."

"I don't want to be in control tonight, Saint," Noel tells me. "I want you to control my body, to control my mind. I want you to decide if and when I come—if I've been a good enough girl for you."

Leaning over her body, I kiss her again, unable to get enough of the peppermint lip gloss she religiously slicks over her pouty lips. Between the body wash and the lip gloss, it's enough to overwhelm the senses, a total aromatherapy experi-ence courtesy of the naked woman in front of me.

Pulling away from her is hard. Part of me wants nothing more than to untie Holly—to bring her cinnamon scent to bed next to us–and to spend the entire evening making out with both women like teenagers in the backseat of my father's fancy car as both tantalizing aromas float around on the air around us like cookies fresh and hot from the oven. But if Noel wants me to take control, to take the lead, that's exactly what I'm going to do.

On the outside, at least.

Noel doesn't need to know that ultimately, she's still the one calling the shots. That she's still the one that can make any of us stop at any time. That I might push her to the brink of screaming her safe word, but that it is never my intention to make her use it.

Everything that was once on the kitchen table is now sitting in a neat row across the head of the mattress, and it brings me pause, wondering when it appeared in the room as if transported by the ghost of Christmas Present.

Well, then call me Ebenezer Fucking Scrooge and haunt my ass till the New Year.

"I brought it all up when you were outside," Noel says quietly, as if not wanting to break the silent yet electric energy humming in the room. "I'm still green."

Not being able to hold myself back any longer, I slide a finger through her slit, her arousal already thick and warm as it coats me. "There are so many things I want to do to you, Baby Girl. So many ways I want to punish you for the torture you put me through for years—for fucking *years*. I want to spank that pretty bottom for parading around in next to nothing." I sink two fingers inside her cunt, viciously and forcefully. "I want to leave bite marks on your skin so anyone who looks at you knows that you've been marked by your filthy stepbrother."

Noel's back bows off the bed, a strangled cry leaving her mouth. From across the room, I catch sight of Holly, her pristinely waxed cunt again beginning to show the telltale signs of her own slick arousal.

Reaching toward the top of the mattress with the hand that

isn't working its way in and out of Noel's pussy, I pick up the scarf—the first item I presented to her downstairs. Amazingly, it feels like another lifetime ago entirely, not something that occurred only hours ago. Without waiting for her to speak another word, I shove the scarf inside her mouth, pushing as much of it into her as possible without choking her on the fabric. "The only problem with that, Baby Girl, is that I can't punish you for something that you did all those years ago. It wouldn't be fair of me to do that to you. But that sure as hell doesn't mean I'm not going to enjoy everything I'm about to do to you. Every spank I leave against that ass of yours tonight isn't in punishment. Every nip and bite isn't designed to make you feel like I'm angry or upset with you. Every single thing I do to your body tonight is to bring you closer and closer to a place you've never been before. A place only I can take you."

Without another glance, I pick up the next item from the mattress, watching with rapt attention as my sister's eyes go wide.

ELEVEN

"Fuck!" Noel's voice calls out, muffled by the fabric still bunched between her lips.

I bring the plastic paddle brush down over her breast again, the flat backside of it striking my stepsister right on top of her sensitive nipple. Nowhere near hard enough to leave any substantial marks, it's still a sensation that she's unaccustomed to. Though the way her body moves into each swat—almost as if she's trying to throw herself into the impact—makes me believe she's enjoying it more than she's letting on.

From across the room, Holly lets out a delighted giggle—a fucking *giggle*—and it makes me start to wonder what other secrets the kinky little minx is hiding. "Enjoying yourself over there, Ms. Yule?"

Momentarily dropping the hairbrush, I work my way through the double-sided dildos and vibrators in differing sizes until I find one with a large, bulbous head. A long, white wire is attached to one end of the device, a small remote dangling from the opposite end.

Leaning into Noel's space, I remove the scarf from her mouth. Gently placing a kiss on the corner of her mouth, I make sure my voice can only be heard by my sister. "You want to see something *really* fun?"

Her nod is eager, a happy grin plastered on her already sex-drunk face.

Pressing against the mattress to rise, I walk over to Holly, picking up the last strand of garland I made sure to leave untouched for just this very reason.

Noel turns herself over on the mattress, but I don't chide her. Knowing that this night is about her, if she wants to watch what's about to happen next, then by all means, I'll let her watch. Propping her chin in her hands as she lays on her stomach, she looks past me and into the eyes of the woman she loves.

"Hey, Baby," Holly addresses Noel lazily—as if she's sitting on a beach drinking margaritas and not strung up like a fucking erotic Christmas piñata. "You look good over there. Real good."

She's not wrong.

Noel's hair has completely fallen from the elastic it was in earlier, her wild curls making her look even more thoroughly worked over than she's already been. Her cheeks are rosy, as if she spent the afternoon in the bitter cold, building a snowman, and her green eyes are as clear as I think I've ever seen them.

She's so fucking beautiful that it sends a physical ache into the deepest recesses of my chest.

It's like somehow between my arrival yesterday and the very moment we're in right now, a flip was switched, and instead of constantly battling against one another, we learned that we could be so much more powerful if we simply worked together.

And I think we have Holly to thank for that.

Our own little Christmas miracle.

I make quick work of the last strand of garland. Red—just like the rest—this one has tiny specks of gold and silver interspersed throughout as if it was made for this specific job—to highlight something so erotic and beautiful that it makes my mouth salivate. Managing to slide my hand with the garland around Holly's torso, I loop the material around her waist, grinning as she laughs from the sensation of the garland against her body once again.

But I know she won't be laughing much longer.

With the wand vibrator in hand, I tie the other end of the garland around the section of the wand that separates the handle from the vibrating tip before placing it against her sensitive clit and making a few final ties. Essentially, Holly now wears a harness, though instead of having something attached to her to penetrate someone else, she will be forced to feel the vibrations of the toy for as long as I decide she should.

The cord that leads to the remote is long, but not quite long enough for what I have planned. Once making sure that Holly is still comfortable and secure with that pretty pussy still on display, I drag her—chair and all—closer to the edge of the bed until she is almost cunt to face with where my sister lays. They line up almost perfectly, as if the chair and bed were designed to work in tandem for just this event.

Noel's eyes are wide as I place the remote in front of her and something akin to power flashes behind her eyes for the briefest of seconds before she turns her head to look at me with a questioning gaze.

"Merry Christmas Eve," I tell her with a wink, pointing to the much more modern clock that adorns the wall on the far side of this bedroom.

The clock rolls over to midnight, and as it does, my sister turns the dial on the remote, a gentle, low hum filling the space between us.

"God, yeeeesss," she moans, turning the simple, one-syllable word into something erotic.

Leaning into her, I pinch a nipple before giving the strewn goddess a kiss. "Nah, Little Girl, it's Saint."

She throws her head back and laughs, stopping only when my sister changes the speed of the device pressed up against her clit.

I walk back to the bed, procuring a few wooden clothespins, before returning to Holly. And as the vibrator lightly whirrs away, I give the clothespin a few squeezes, watching as the two pieces separate from one another before coming back together with a quiet little click. It's a total bro move—one that any man who has ever picked up a drill or a pair of tongs has done—yet I can't help it from happening.

Holly continues to squirm against her ties while watching me as I return to her side, never getting pressure exactly where she wants—just as intended. I trail a clothespin up her stomach, teasing across her collarbone and down her arm before opening it once again. This time, when it closes, it does so around her pink nipple.

Chuckling at the noise she makes, I repeat the process on her other breast, all the while continuing the playful touches I drag up and down her exposed skin.

"Imagine how one of these would feel against your clit."

Her whimper in response is only encouraged as Noel once again changes the speed of the vibrator.

It's interesting, splitting my time between the two women while trying not to leave one out of the fun. Sure, I've had my time alone with each of them today, but this experience—this is about coming together as a trio. Coming together as three separate bodies to create a powerful force of pleasure and elation enough to shake the cosmos off balance.

Good thing for all of us, despite what women will claim to the contrary about most men, I'm a master multi-tasker.

Taking a step back, I admire my handy work.

And what a fucking beautiful scene it is.

Holly is still tied to the chair, legs spread wide. Though now, where both Noel and I previously had a direct line of sight to her pussy, she's obscured by the large head of the toy pressed against her slit. Each nipple is clamped carefully by a clothespin, and the most beautiful sheen of sweat has begun to break out across her sinful body.

Climbing back onto the bed, I now take my place behind Noel, urging her onto her hands and knees while keeping her facing toward her lover.

"You're a lucky woman," I tell her honestly. "And so is she. You're both beautiful and intelligent, but together—you're Goddamned breathtaking."

Trailing a finger down her spine, I press her face into the mattress while leaving her ass high in the air. Like a honing beacon calling me home, I bend into her, biting her on the left cheek—like I've been fantasizing about doing for longer than I care to admit.

In response, she shrieks into the otherwise quiet room before breaking into a fit of laughter. "Saint!" She whines my name, and it's the cutest fucking thing I've ever heard. "That hurt!"

Leaning over her body with my large frame, I gently tap the remote she is still grasping, urging her to turn the dial up another notch. Before pushing back to a kneeling position, I lick up the shell of her ear, speaking for her alone. "It's supposed to hurt, Baby Girl. But that's what makes it feel all that much better in the end. The pain, the anticipation of when and where on your body it will come next, the way you'll come to *crave* it over time."

Missing her heat the moment I move away from her body, I reclaim my spot behind her on the mattress. With one hand flat against the small of her back, I hold her in place while picking up the hairbrush in my other.

Noel's body tenses, surely expecting me to take the backside of the brush to her gorgeous ass. But instead, I use the side normally reserved for combing out unruly tresses, and drag the bristles up and down her spine. I run the brush over the globes of her ass, increasing the pressure I use with each and every caress.

At first, she squirms against the sensation before melting into the feel of the bristles against her skin. Keeping up the ruse, I run the brush over any exposed flesh I can find. Over the backs of her legs and her ticklish feet, her long, graceful arms and even lightly over the sides of her neck. And when she thinks that this is all I'm going to give her—that I'm going to continue this tease with careful, gentle strokes—I press into the brush with some force behind it, changing the sensation from a light tickle to a firm pressure that leaves tiny pinpricks on her skin as I drag it back down her lithe body toward her ass.

From her place in the chair, Holly watches, her eyes darting between Noel's face, my hand carefully carving a path over my sister's body, and my own face. And when we catch one another's eye, she smiles. In response, I toss a wink in her direction, just as I see Noel bump up the speed on the toy another notch.

I watch as Holly's head falls back against the wooden chair, an audible *thunk* filling the room as the two connect. I watch as her legs strain against the garland that keeps her tied tightly in place, and I watch her toes curl as the toy pressed against her sex takes her closer and closer to the edge.

And Goddamn, do I want to watch her as she tips over that edge.

Returning my full attention to Noel—her ass still so prettily on display—I give her one swift smack with the back side of the brush, loving the low groan that vibrates through her body.

"More," she pants. "I can take more."

Giving her exactly what she's asked for, I smack her ass again, reveling in the way her breath catches. In the way her normally smooth and creamy skin ripples before lightly pinking from the impact. It's too tempting, to reach out and touch her skin with nothing but my hand, and I find myself tossing the brush aside before my palm connects with my sister's ass.

She squirms as I run my hands over her ass, massaging at the tender flesh. Noel's face drops to the mattress as I spread her cheeks wide, admiring the forbidden hole that I can't wait to sink my dick into. Unexpectedly, when I lean down and lick her in the very same place, she doesn't shy away, pushing her greedy, little ass further against my face. And when I pull back, quickly giving her one hard smack across her ass, she screams my name while pressing the button on the remote that will send our Holly one step closer to release.

Yeah, that's right.

Not her Holly.

Ours.

Because here, in this moment, I know I'm determined to keep both of these women in my life for way longer than one night.

No matter what it takes.

TWELVE

"I need to be inside one of you in the next five minutes, or I'm going to lose my fucking mind."

Moving from my place behind Noel, I take the remote from her hand, turning the dial down to nothing more than a low hum and placing it on the bed next to her.

Pulling her into my arms, our lips crash together in a frenzy as if it's been years since I last kissed her instead of mere minutes. "I can't get enough of you." I rasp before turning to look at Holly. "Either of you."

Both women watch as I make fast work of the ties keeping the vibrator secure against Holly's cunt, and when it's finally free, I toss it on the bed, not caring when it bounces once and falls onto the floor.

Gesturing to my sister, I urge her closer. "Look how wet you made her."

"Not just me. It was us. *Together*." Her response is soft—almost as soft as the smile playing across her lips. But neverthe-less, it's there, and like everything else about Noel, it's magnificent.

I run my hand through Noel's curls, gently pulling when my

fingers get tangled in the tresses. "Want to do something else together?"

"Haven't you realized it yet, Saint? I'd do anything with you —anything *for* you." Noel's voice is even softer now. For the first time today, she sounds more like the young woman she still is and not the eighteen-year-old socialite she has been groomed to be.

It's a tender moment in the middle of something so chaotically erotic, yet I take the time to answer her just as earnestly, knowing she deserves my truth at the very least. "I'm starting to realize it, Baby Girl. I'm just sorry it took me so long. I'm sorry that I pushed you away for so long, that I treated you as my enemy. All I can do is to spend every day of the rest of my life trying to make it up to you. I just hope one day, you can truly forgive me."

Noel looks at me, tears and mischief dancing in her eyes in a strangely heady combination of relief and arousal. "You've already been forgiven. Now show me what else we can do together, Daddy."

Without waiting for her to take another breath, I push her head forward into Holly's pussy, watching as she goes willingly.

Like the greedy little girl she is, she dips her chin, licking up the length of Holly's cunt before fully burying her face between the spread legs of her lover.

In response, Holly moans–a guttural sound that comes from deep within the recesses of her soul. "Goddamn. It's about time the two of you finally learned to work together."

Leaning over, I flick one of the clothespins still attached to Holly's nipple, laughing as she gasps from the sensation. "Watch your mouth or I'll take my sister right the fuck out of this room and leave you here all wet and needy. Your cunt bare and on display with absolutely no way for you to find relief."

Noel pulls back, chin glistening from Holly's arousal that has been smeared across her face. She's so beautiful—a debauched goddess sent from the heavens with the sole intent of driving me wild. "That would be equally mean to me, Saint. And you don't want to make your darling Baby Girl sad, do you? We've come so far over the last day, it would be a shame to slip back into old habits so quickly."

"Brats," I tell them. "You're both fucking brats." This time, when I say it, it's filled with laughter and lightness—none of the ill-placed hatred I had for these two women only a short time ago.

I reclaim my place behind my sister, finally removing the shirt and sleep pants I've been wearing up until this moment. All the while, I watch as Holly's eyes track each and every move I make with a slow, approving perusal of her piercing, blue eyes.

Each of these women have already gotten me off separately today, but now, with both of them together and naked in the same room, I feel like I could combust from the electricity in the air alone.

Crawling behind my sister, I urge her to spread her knees wider apart, her ass still high in the air while her face is back at work, sucking and lapping at Holly's cunt. I drag my dick through her folds, wetting myself thoroughly before notching myself against her ass.

And when she gives a little whimper, I smack her ass. "Just kidding, Baby Girl. Daddy doesn't want to hurt you too badly. We'll work you up to taking my cock back there so we can fulfill that fantasy of yours."

With that, I angle my hips, sliding into her cunt with one thrust.

Noel is slick and wet, and I slide in easily, yet she's still the tightest fucking thing that I've ever been inside. Her walls tense around the intrusion, squeezing me to within an inch of my life. "Christ, Baby. Keep that up and I'm going to come before we even get started."

She pulls her head away from Holly long enough to call over her shoulder, "Greedy. You better not come before me."

As she tries to lower her head back, I grab a fistful of her hair, pulling her upright against my chest while wrapping my other arm around her waist. The cry she lets out into the room sets me on fire. "Keep talking like that and I'll have to give you a time-out."

I'm still buried inside her cunt, able to feel her pulse around me with every small movement I make—with every small thrust of my hips and every filthy word that drips from my tongue. "Keep acting like you're in control, and I'll never let you come. I'll just push you to the edge again and again, ruining that orgasm you want so badly every fucking time. Every single time you think it's just within your reach, I'll pull it away from you again."

Holly's eyes are dark as the sea during a raging storm as she watches—her own needy cunt and my sister's saliva dripping onto the chair beneath where she is tied.

"What about you?" I ask her. "Do you deserve relief? Do you think you deserve to come, to watch the stars explode behind your eyes as you scream out my name?"

Her smile is lazy. "That's not for me to decide, is it?"

"See, Baby?" I ask my sister, still lazily thrusting inside her the entire time. "That's how you act.

The transformation Holly has undergone from when she was my caregiver not that long ago—pulling me back from the edge of a dangerous, rage-fueled cliff—in a more dominant way to the more submissive role she has taken on now is incredible. A true switch, able to swiftly move through roles as both a top and bottom while in the middle of a scene, it's like watching a caterpillar transform into a butterfly before my very eyes.

I'm truly beginning to believe that this entire time, she was the missing piece.

One hand still around my sister's torso, I reach behind me

with the other, sliding my hand across the mattress until I once again have the scarf in my hand.

With a few simple movements, I have it slipped around my sister's wrists in a simple, double-column tie. Sliding out of the warmth of her pussy, I wrap a loose end over the nearest of the four posters that jut up from each corner of the bed. With a messy kiss to her lips, I leave the bed, padding my way to Holly as she watches me with rapt attention. "See what happens when you behave, Noel? When you behave like a good girl, you get orgasms."

Starting with Holly's legs, I untie the knots holding her to the chair, gently massaging her skin as I work in reverse of what I previously did until her legs are able to move on their own accord once again. Working in silence—Noel's eyes on us the entire time—it's almost like I'm unwrapping my very own Christmas present, one my sister only wishes she could get her hands on.

Once Holly's safely untied, I lead her to the bed, laying her back on the thick down comforter. Her head turns toward where I stand off to the side, waiting for my next move.

"See, Baby," my attention is still on my sister, even as I trail my fingers up and down Holly's bare skin. One by one, I remove the clothespins from her nipples, leaning down to lick and lave each tight bud with my tongue as the blood flows back into the sensitive peaks. "When you're a good girl, I'll touch you again." I easily slide two fingers inside of Holly, feeling her in this intimate way for the first time. Her mouth falls open on a moan, and I take the opportunity to glide myself to her mouth. "Now, Holly, sweetheart, tell me how my sweet sister tastes on my cock."

With gusto, she brings her head to meet my dick, easily opening her mouth to allow me entrance. I don't know if she's more excited to suck my cock or to taste Noel on my skin, but either way, I'm not going to complain. I continue to pump into her with my fingers, adding a third and loving the way she stretches for me so pliantly as I slide in and out of her mouth with slow, easy strokes.

My sister continues to watch, her mouth parted in a small, sated smile.

But a small, sated smile certainly won't work tonight.

No, I won't stop with either of them until they're in a heap of boneless flesh on the floor.

THIRTEEN

With my cock buried in Holly's mouth, my fingers equally as deep in her cunt, I use the one free hand I have to reach toward my sister, pulling at the loose end of the scarf that has been tied to the post.

It falls to the bed, my sister's still-bound hands falling as well.

Expecting her to move, to immediately make her way to where Holly and I are, I'm pleasantly surprised when she stays where she is, awaiting my next command.

"Crawl your beautiful body over, here and I'll give you a reward," I tell her, waiting to see if she'll obey.

She looks at me with a look of pure exasperation before looking down to her bound hands. "How the fuck do you expect me to do that?"

I give the side of Holly's face a light tap, waiting for her to pop off my dick. A trail of saliva hangs from the side of her mouth, dribbling down her chin. Swiping it away with my thumb, I push the spit back into her mouth before moving to the head of the bed.

Instructing Holly without words, I gesture for her to join me, positioning her with her ass facing Noel. Smacking her on the ass, I then slide my hand between her legs, spreading the wetness over her folds.

Finally turning my attention back to my sister, I meet her pissed-off stare with one of my own. "Figure it out and you'll get your reward. In the meantime, I'll just be sitting here, playing with this beautiful cunt."

I watch the wheels in her head as they spin, catching her as I see a plan forming. "And don't even think about putting your feet on that floor. You want me—want what I'm going to give you—then you're going to crawl to me like the filthy girl you are."

She sits back on a *harrumph*, pissed that I already foiled her plans.

Long moments pass as I sit patiently, waiting for her to make her next move. All the while, I continue to tease Holly's pussy while giving myself long, leisurely strokes.

Noel watches Holly. She watches as my fingers disappear inside her girlfriend over and over again. She watches as I reach between Holly's legs, coming away with a hand wet with her arousal, before I wrap the same hand around my length again.

Need finally wins out over the potential humiliation, and I watch my sister as she tries her hardest to crawl across the length of the bed with her hands still bound in front of her. Like a little inchworm, her ass comes up in the air before she pulls herself forward. Again and again, she completes the move, pushing and pulling and pushing and pulling, until finally, she's just a few inches away.

Grabbing the scarf wrapped around her wrists, I pull her on top of me, being sure not to pull too harshly against the material. Temporary marks may be sexy as hell, but I refuse to cause any lasting harm to my beautiful sister.

I wrap a hand around the back of her neck, bringing her forehead to rest against mine "You might not think it, Baby Girl, but your submission is the sexiest thing I think I've ever seen in my life. The way you crawled over here to me—to us...it was beautiful. Knowing you did it to please me..." I thrust my hips once, letting her feel just how hard I am as my cock slides against her entrance.

The praise melts the icy demeanor that had been creeping back in around the edges, placating her inner brat. "Does that mean I get my reward now?"

Bringing the hand that had been toying with Holly to my sister's lips, I slip them inside, groaning as she greedily sucks my fingers. "Yeah, Princess, you can have your reward now."

I kiss Noel, tasting Holly on her lips.

From next to me, Holly moves, shifting into a sitting position with her back against the headboard, her legs spread as wide as she can. Noel climbs off my lap and sits between Holly's outstretched legs, her back to Holly's front.

And while there is nothing I would love more than to line them up, slamming into one pussy before sliding into the second over and over, Holly was clear that full penetration was off the table for her and gave explicit instructions that while I could toy with her all I wanted, she didn't want to come.

Deranged? Possibly. But who I am to choose what she does and doesn't get off on? Besides, I'm nothing if not a gentleman when it comes to hard limits.

Finally, I take my place, kneeling in front of Noel while Holly holds her from behind. Bypassing Noel's beautiful face, I lean into Holly, claiming her with a kiss before repeating the same thing with my sister. I watch as the two share their own kiss—softer than the one we each just shared, yet not any less passionate.

If I've learned anything since stumbling upon Noel in the hot tub, it's that both she and Holly have a love that runs deep for one another. That their relationship was built on solid ground, and that perhaps talking and communication has its place outside of only being used for business and kink negotiations.

It's something I'm determined to work on. Something that I hope helps me to build a strong bond with both of these women, who I already feel responsible for in a way I'm unaccustomed to feeling.

And tomorrow morning, I'm thinking of asking them for more.

Slotting myself against Noel's entrance, I sink in slowly. Committing the feeling to memory on the off chance this truly is a one-time thing. I've used her cunt and have stretched her with my fingers, yet I'm still gentle—still cautious of being too much all at once.

Inch after delicious inch, I work my way inside, sliding out before reentering her in long, languid strokes. I watch as I slide in and out, her arousal slick and shiny on my cock. And when I see the look of awe on Holly's face as she watches where her girlfriend and I join together—when I see how enraptured she is by the act—I'm almost glad that she decided to watch without wanting more for herself, that she allowed herself to fulfill one of her own deepest desires of watching the act while giving Noel one of her own fantasies as well.

I lean forward, holding myself up with palms against the headboard as my speed picks up, and when Holly's hand comes out to grasp onto my bicep, her nails digging into my flesh, I nearly come undone.

"Tell me if it's too rough, if it's too much, and we can change positions," I manage to grit out, aware that with each thrust of my hips, I'm pushing my sister into Holly with increasing thrust.

She never tears her eyes away from our bodies, never stops looking from my arms to chest, to Noel's perky tits that bounce, and back to the place where I slide into Noel's cunt again and again. "Perfect," she says, her voice strained as if she's approaching her own climax without even being touched, as if she is truly enjoying this just as much as me and Noel are.

Holly's free arm, the one not tearing through my skin with her talons, slides down my sister's neck. Lower and lower, she travels until she is able to palm one breast, pinching her nipple hard enough to make Noel cry out. But her hand doesn't stay still, continuing on a southern trajectory until she settles between my sister's legs, finding her clit with greedy, little fingers.

"Open your eyes, Baby Girl."

My sister stutters out a response, her eyes opening to meet mine. "There's so much sensation. So many extra hands and limbs."

A bead of sweat rolls down my temple before falling onto Noel's skin, and while I speak, I never slow the relentless pace I've worked up to. "If you need me to slow down or stop, you just say the word."

"Green."

It's all she says.

One word with endless opportunity.

Opportunity I've only reached the surface of exploring with these two Christmas angels brought to life.

Feeling Noel's cunt as it begins to tighten ever further around my cock, I look down to watch as Holly toys with her clit, occasionally bumping into my dick with her fingers. It's gentle despite the force I put behind each thrust, her soft skin barely grazing my own.

And I fucking *love* it.

Noel keens, her voice filling the room around us like a choir filling a church on Christmas Eve. I urge Holly to keep rubbing, to keep tormenting Noel's pussy.

"She's so close," I tell her. "Like a Goddamned vice grip on my cock."

Holly's pupils dilate, confirming she's enjoying this just as much as I am. "Send her over the edge, Saint. Give our girl what she wants."

I look to Holly, something passing silently between us in the moment. It's a promise of more, a promise of what's to come. And I can't fucking wait.

The headboard slams against the wall with each thrust, and I'm about damned sure that I'm going to have to pay to have the room patched up when we get done with it. Again and again, I slam into Noel as Holly continues to tease her clit. And just when I think that I can barely hold on another second, my beautiful stepsister calls out my name before wave after wave of her orgasm crashes into her body, setting my own release off in a chain reaction.

I roar as my release fills her, then crash my lips against hers as the spots slowly begin to fade from behind my eyes. My head falls to a space between her body and Holly's—all of us having shifted during the last several minutes—and when I feel fingers trailing through my short hair, I look up to see a smiling Holly staring at me with reverence on her beautiful face.

Rolling off my sister with a small kiss to her forehead, I climb from the bed, knowing from the beginning, Holly would be the one in charge of aftercare—of making sure Noel felt safe, secure, and loved after the events we planned. The events that *I* planned. That at the time of our negotiations, this was planned to be one night and one night only.

What I don't expect is for the hollowness that I feel in my chest as I begin to dress.

Chancing a look at the two women as I approach the door, I see that Holly has already pulled warm blankets over my sister's body. That she is uncapping a bottle of water and holding it to Noel's lips.

Just as I'm about to close the door, to leave them alone, a voice stops me in my tracks.

"You said you'd never run away again." Noel sounds so

small. So timid and broken. "Would it be so wrong if you just decided to stay? To give us—both of us—a try?"

Every moment I've ever shared with her flashes before my eyes as if it's my last moments on Earth. The first day she bounced her way into my life with those lively curls and even livelier attitude. All the times she stubbornly pushed my buttons in an attempt to become closer to me without knowing she was actually pushing me further away. Each tiny, little outfit that she wore to tempt me, and that night in the pool house—the first time she called me *Daddy*.

I stand there, hand poised on the doorknob while torn between the two options, my heart beating loudly in my chest as if teasing me on with a cadence of *do it...do it...do it*.

It doesn't take long for me to make the decision, all of Holly's words from earlier today—about being alone and afraid and desperate for family–come back to me. I know it's exactly what I've been desperate for my entire life, too.

And it's all just on the other side of that door, waiting for me.

Fuck our parents, who did more harm than good by leaving us all to our own devices when we needed them most. And fuck society if they cannot accept that I can have such strong feelings for not one but two people after such a short time, one of which is my sister only through marriage.

Everyone can take their Goddamned standards and norms and shove them up their asses. Because just on the other side of that door—my entire life awaits.

Throwing the door open, I stride to the bed, two pairs of wide eyes meeting mine as I do. I see the trepidation in both of their faces, the uncertainty and fear. It makes me want to kick my own ass for putting that doubt on their faces.

Without saying another word, I do the only thing I can think of knowing that come morning, we'll have a ton of shit to figure out, but that for now, I'll just focus on tonight.

Pulling back the blankets, I crawl into bed with my two Christmas miracles, press kisses to each of their lips, which I hope conveys the seriousness of my intent, and vow silently that this is only the first of many holidays we'll spend together.

Because now that I know how good it can be, I know that all I want for Christmas...is two.

-THE END-

OTHER WORKS

Broken Sparrow Collection:

Inked

Etched

Luna Sea Plaza:

Sew Into You

Standalone Books:

The Arrangement

Beautiful Games

Knotty Valentine (Sapphic Novella)

ABOUT
AMITY

Amity Malcom was born in Pennsylvania. She began writing short stories while still in elementary school-including a total page turner about how her mother loved to fish. Her mother does not love to fish and is actually terrified by ocean creatures.

She now resides in Florida with her wife, two completely insane but lovable cats and one neurotic but adorable dog.

When not writing steamy characters and happily ever afters, Amity can be found watching professional soccer, exploring Florida's many theme parks, and campaigning for LGBTQIA+ rights.

SOCIAL MEDIA

Instagram

Facebook Page

Facebook Reader Group

Join Amity's Newsletter

TikTok

www.ingramcontent.com/pod-product-compliance
Lightning Source LLC
Chambersburg PA
CBHW072008170626
46813CB00005B/2070